DEATH AT BETHESDA FALLS

Jim Thorp did not relish this visit to Bethesda Falls. His old sweetheart Anna worked there and he was hunting her brother Clyde, the foreman of the M-bar-W ranch. Her brother is due to wed Ellen, the rancher's daughter. He is also poisoning the old man to hasten the inheritance. Thorp's presence in town starts the downward slide into violence . . . and danger for Anna, Ellen and Thorp himself. It is destined to end in violence and death.

ROSS MORTON

DEATH AT BETHESDA FALLS

Complete and Unabridged

LINFORD
Leicester

First published in Great Britain in 2007 by
Robert Hale Limited
London

First Linford Edition
published 2008
by arrangement with
Robert Hale Limited
London

British Library CIP Data

Morton, Ross
  Death at Bethesda Falls.—Large print ed.—
Linford western library
  1. Western stories
  2. Large type books
  I. Title
  823.9'2 [F]

  ISBN 978–1–84782–432–5

Published by
F. A. Thorpe (Publishing)
Anstey, Leicestershire

Set by Words & Graphics Ltd.
Anstey, Leicestershire
Printed and bound in Great Britain by
T. J. International Ltd., Padstow, Cornwall

This book is printed on acid-free paper

1

Rue the Lash

James Thorp eased his sorrel horse to a halt on the outskirts of the small town of Bethesda Falls, which nestled at the base of the mountain's foothills. He was dressed entirely in black. Black because he was in mourning. Mourning the men he had killed.

Every movement that he made in the saddle was slow and considered. He rested the hand that held the reins on the pommel and with his free hand nudged the flat brim, pushing the flat-crowned hat to the back of his head. He used his silk neckerchief to wipe the sweat from his tanned and lined brow; his weathered features suggested that he was a lot older than his twenty-six years.

The signboard at the side of the road announced:

WELCOME TO
BETHESDA FALLS
FOUNDED 1858
POP. ~~412~~ 411.

If his last informant was square, then he would be giving whoever painted that sign the job of reducing the population count by yet one more.

No great loss to the world, he opined, gently urging the sorrel towards the livery stable at the end of the main street, over on the right.

Like so many similar small towns that were springing up in Dakota Territory, Bethesda Falls comprised a long main street with a small cluster of buildings forming short side streets that spread east and west. There was a strong hint of more expansion on the east side, with two new buildings half-completed; so, even after only eight years of life, the town was clearly flourishing. At the north end, tinted a rose glow from the dying sun, loomed Grimm Mountain, while to Thorp's left were cultivated fields sloping down towards Clearwater Creek and several smaller water courses.

Thorp reined in at Zachary's Livery and slowly swung his leg over his saddlebags and tarp-covered bedroll and stepped down. He almost sensed the ache ease out of his bones as he felt the firm ground under his hand-tooled boots. The bullwhip tied to his belt knocked gently against his thigh. He adjusted his weapons belt, tied down the two holsters, then looped the reins over the hitching rail.

From here he could see a fair portion of the corral at the back. A big man on foot was tugging at the bridle of a splendid specimen of a palomino. The man was broad-shouldered and swearing at the horse, angrily cracking his whip on the ground.

'Stayin' long, mister?' asked an old-timer who stepped out from the shadows of the livery's half-open double doors.

'Maybe just overnight,' Thorp responded.

The livery man's hand rasped over his chinwhiskers as he chewed. 'Business in town?'

'Maybe. I'm looking for someone. Heard he lived here.'

The man's screwed-up eyes lingered on Thorp's two Remington Navy model six-guns which were slung low and slantwise. He also took in the sheathed Bowie-knife. 'Is that so?' Spitting a gobbet of tobacco juice into the dust, he neatly changed the subject: 'Fine horseflesh you have there, mister.'

'Thanks. I came into some luck.' Thorp decided not to mention that the luck of the sorrel's owner had run out. He turned his attention back to the corral.

The old man noticed Thorp eyeing the palomino and its irate handler. 'Never mind Tom Durey, he has a chip on his shoulder.'

'No need to take it out on that fine horse.'

'I couldn't agree more, mister, but I ain't up to chastisin' such a big feller.'

'No, I suppose not.' Thorp walked along the side of the livery building and above the sound of his spurs he heard the shuffling gait of the old man following behind.

Thorp stopped and leaned on a corral rail, narrow slate-grey eyes studying Tom Durey.

A mite taller than Thorp, at about six-two, Durey was not a man to be easily chastised. His arms and thighs carried big muscles but he was also laden down with a load of lard round his midriff, where his red checked shirt bulged. His straggly long brown hair and beard intimated that Durey was not quite tame. Maybe he, too, needed breaking in. His left eye was half-closed, a scar tracing its way from brow to chin. His right eye was dark brown and glared maliciously at the stallion as he cracked the whip.

Understandably displeased, the palomino reared up. A thin red welt appeared on its golden flank. Its eyes wide, the animal snorted and tugged, but Durey was a heavy and strong man and wasn't going to let go so easily.

Thorp sighed, unfastened his bullwhip and ducked under the lodgepole rail and stood upright in the corral. Normally quite faint, the scar on his left temple was now livid.

'This I'm thinkin' I'm gonna like,' the old man whispered behind him.

Before Durey could thrash the palomino again, Thorp's bullwhip snaked out and lashed itself around Durey's wrist. Bracing himself against a corral post, Thorp tugged and Durey abruptly let go of the palomino's reins as he tried to prevent himself from being dragged through the dirt.

'What the hell?' Durey exclaimed, head turning to the owner of the bullwhip.

'Hell is where you're going, Durey,' Thorp snarled, 'if you continue mistreating horses like that!'

The palomino backed off and snorted, head down, studying Durey and then

Thorp. A shiver ran through its body and it shook itself, the flaxen mane coruscating in the last rays of the sinking sun.

Durey unravelled Thorp's whip and lowered his head into his shoulders, telegraphing that he was about to charge. 'You made a big mistake, stranger, tanglin' with me!' Growling like a cougar on heat, he ran at Thorp, head down, close-set eyes in shadow, his own whip in one hand, a swiftly unsheathed hunting knife in the other.

With a lithe motion, Thorp side-stepped to the right and stuck out his foot. Durey tripped and sprawled in the dust. Thorp cracked his bullwhip down hard, the tip tearing the man's shirt at the shoulder and breaking the skin. Flinching with pain, Durey dropped his knife.

'If you want a matching scar for the other eye, just keep right on charging me,' Thorp advised.

Holding his cut shoulder, Durey growled, 'You haven't heard the last of this, stranger!'

He doubted if he'd heard that worn-out phrase for the last time, either. 'No need to consider me a stranger. The name's Thorp. Jim Thorp.'

'It'll sit well on your tombstone!'

'I'm real obliged you want to contribute, even if you're a mite premature.' He bowed, grinning broadly. 'If you can spell,' he added, speaking very slowly, 'it's James Dexter Thorp.'

'Go to hell!'

'Very likely. But not before you, I reckon.'

'You bastard, you've no right to interfere when a man is training a crockhead!'

'You don't train a horse with a whip. In fact, you don't deserve that horse.'

'Oh, yeah? And you're going to buy it off of me, are you?'

'Maybe. How much?'

'More'n you could afford, Thorp.'

'Mr Thorp!' called the old livery man.

Durey took advantage of the interruption and rose to his feet and dusted down his pants.

Thorp strode over to the livery man on the other side of the corral poles, mindful of Durey's actions. Whispering, the man told him what the palomino had cost. Nodding, Thorp dug into his pocket and flung a few bank notes at Durey's feet. 'The deal's done, Durey. I advise you to take it and get out of town.'

'You ain't no sheriff!'

'No, but I'm sure losing patience with you. I've just come off the trail and I'm tired and hungry. And if I don't get a bath and some food soon, I'm liable to get real irritable.'

'So, what's that to me?'

'You don't want to see me irritable,' Thorp said, his tone like ice.

Durey growled something unintelligible under his breath and collected the money. He hastily counted it and arched his unblemished eyebrow at Thorp, perhaps surprised that he hadn't been short-changed. His brow crinkled and his good eye glared. 'Bastard!' He bent down to reach for his fallen whip; he wasn't fool enough to pick up his knife.

Thorp's bullwhip cracked against the ground, sending dirt into Durey's face. 'When I hear you're treating horses with proper respect, I might consider returning that whip to you. Not before!'

Scowling, Tom Durey backed off. Then he lumbered towards town, occasionally glaring over his shoulder.

'You sure didn't make a friend there, Mr Thorp,' said the old man as they walked back to the front of Zachary's Livery.

'I doubt if he has many friends anyway.'

'Well, I'd like to shake your hand. It isn't every day I see that bully bested!'

As they shook hands, the old man asked, 'What do you want me to do with the palomino?'

Taking off his hat, Thorp ran a hand through his burnt-almond hair. 'I don't rightly know. I must admit I hadn't intended getting a second horse. Maybe I could start up a pony express business?'

'Nope. You'd need more mounts than two.'

He made a mental note not to use irony on the old-timer in future. 'Well, take care of him till I decide what to do, will you?'

'Sure, mister. That should be two dollars but I won't charge for the palomino as that's the best evenin's entertainment I've had in a long while.'

'Thanks.' Thorp handed over a dollar.

He pocketed the money. 'Are you wantin' to stay at a saloon or a fancy hotel? Neither don't come cheap.'

Thorp ran a hand over the day's whiskers. 'Maybe. What do you recommend?'

'Me, I'm real comfortable with the bed and board provided by Mrs McCall. Her place has a shingle. 'Cherry Tree Boarding Rooms' it's called on account of the cherry tree out front.'

'That'll do me fine. She a good cook?'

'I ain't got no complaints. Better than that fancy hash-house that's opened — they call it a restaurant. Bringing new-fangled food fidfads from back East.'

Thorp pulled his Henry repeating rifle from its saddle-holster. He unfastened his saddlebags and slung them over his broad shoulder. Tonight he had no need of his bedroll. 'I guess I'll see you at dinner?'

'Sure, mister.' He unfastened the reins of Thorp's sorrel. 'I'll just tank up your horse and make him comfortable then I'll be right along. It ain't wise to keep Widow McCall waitin'.' He was about to take Thorp's horse when he hesitated. 'Name's Amos, by the way.' He held out his hand.

For an old-timer he had a strong handshake. Thorp said, 'Amos Zachary?'

'No, Amos Jones. I manage the livery for him — Zachary Smith. He's gone up in the world. Part-owner in The Gem — the saloon on the east side. You don't want to frequent that place. Wet your whistle at El Dorado — much fairer prices . . . '

'Well, I'm real obliged, Amos. My name's Jim.'

'Yeah, I heard.' Amos grinned, as if pleased to be on first-name terms with a man like Thorp. He started to lead the sorrel into the stable. 'See you at dinner, Jim,' he called over his shoulder.

Thorp strode up the street, his rifle gripped in his left hand, his slate-grey eyes slanted to either side of the main street, missing nothing.

There was the usual hotchpotch of false fronts — on the left, the Bella Union, obviously the town's cathouse, with its over-ornate veranda and balconies, where a couple of courtesans displayed red petticoats, frilly garters and a length of leg as they draped themselves enticingly on the rails: he good-naturedly waved away their importuning gestures. On the right, Oren Tatch, Blacksmith; then the El Dorado saloon beckoned, opposite Monroe's Stage Depot.

Thorp stepped up onto the board-walk and pushed open the batwing doors of the saloon.

It was too early in the evening for the place to be full. Besides the barkeep, there were four men playing faro at the back, and on the right, two men sat at a table, jawing over pitchers of beer, while on the left there was a black pianist and a Mexican chanteuse who were murdering some song from back East — that is, until they noticed Thorp in the doorway.

He was used to the silence that followed his entrance into strange rooms. He was tall and broad and didn't carry an ounce of fat. His linen shirt and broadcloth trousers didn't show the sweat-stains, but the fine film of dust clearly announced he had just come in off the trail. He removed his hat and beat it against a leg to dispel some of Dakota's dirt. Several pairs of eyes met his, but only briefly, then glanced away. It was a rare man who stared at James D. Thorp.

The singer and pianist started up again as Thorp dumped his saddlebags and hat on the bar counter. He rested the rifle against the side.

Limping over the duckboards behind the counter, the bartender wore a salt-and-pepper moustache, a fairly white shirt and a lugubrious expression. His face gave the impression that he'd seen and heard it all, but he was game if you wanted to talk. 'What'll it be, stranger?'

'A whiskey and some information, if you'd be so kind.'

The barkeep's shoulders hunched, as if implying that he'd heard that before as well. 'Sure, sir,' he said in a non-committal tone. The shot glass was topped to the brim with the honey-coloured liquor and the bartender expertly slid it smoothly over to Thorp without spilling a drop. 'First one's on the house.'

'Thank you. That's mighty friendly of you.' Thorp drank it in one gulp, the fiery liquid reacquainting his throat

15

with a pleasurable sensation he had hankered after for many lonesome trail days. 'And the information?'

'That'll come free as well, sir, when you buy your next drink.'

Thorp's grin was broad. 'I like your style, barkeep. Make it another one, then.'

As he obliged, the bartender asked, 'What do you want to know, sir?'

'Where can I find the Comstock place?'

'No problem, sir.' The bartender smiled. 'And, seeing as you're a friend of Miss Comstock, I shan't be charging you for your second drink, neither.'

'That's mighty fine of you.' Thorp didn't disabuse the man of his assumption as he sipped his drink. 'Do many men pay court on Miss Comstock?'

'A few have thought on it but she never showed no interest. Dedicated, she is. Our daughter Mabel's doing real fine with her writin'.' A thought creased the bartender's brow and he voiced it: 'You ain't thinkin' of takin' her away from us, are you?'

'No,' Thorp mollified. 'I'm here strictly on business.' Deadly business, but the barkeep didn't need to know that.

* * *

Fit to bursting, Thorp struck a sulphur match against Mrs McCall's veranda post and lit a thin cigar.

Not only on account of his full belly did he stroll a mite slowly down Main Street.

Amos had been right about Mrs McCall's cooking. He had never tasted anything quite like her flank steak with rye whiskey marinade. Who'd have thought of cooking with liquor? Some hard-ass drinkers might quail at the apparent waste, but he wasn't one of them. He reckoned that the meat was too good to have come off a steer, and he told her so. She was pleased to hear it. Then, to finish off, there was her wild berry shortcake; it simply melted on his lips. He barely had room for three cups of Java.

He would have been happy with just one cup of coffee, but he had kept drinking because he was putting off this walk to the end of the street.

Sometimes, he hated what he did. This was one of those times.

With a belly full of good food, fresh from a bath and having had a shave, he almost felt civilized again. Fanciful thought, that, he opined, as killing is not civilized, no how.

Stopping at the white picket-fence that circled the town's schoolhouse, he glanced at the dim yellow light flickering in the upstairs window. He dropped the cigarillo and his boot trod it into the ground. He fished out his father's silver fob timepiece and clicked it open. Ten after ten. Maybe that was late in these parts. Come back tomorrow, he told himself; straight after school's out. His lips pursed. No. Get it over and done with now.

Replacing the fob watch in his

trouser pocket, Thorp quietly unlatched the wooden gate and carefully closed it behind him. He walked past a row of struggling rose plants amidst dry earth and slowly climbed the steps to the veranda. On the left was a rocking chair and a small round table, both carpentered from pine. A kerosene lamp glowed from the veranda ceiling. He pulled the metal ring on the right of the door.

A distant light tinkling noise, maybe coming from the kitchen.

Then a sash window opened noisily above. 'Yes, can I help you?' came a disembodied woman's voice, an edge of irritation laced over a fine gentle timbre. Shades of memory, yet older, more confident, he thought, his heart pounding.

He stepped back off the veranda and raised his hat in greeting. 'Good evening, do I have the honour of addressing Miss Comstock?'

She was in silhouette, stray strands of hair creating a halo round her head.

'Yes, you do, but this is not the time to be selling . . . ' She paused and a hand went up to her mouth. 'Do I know you?'

'You surely do, Anna.'

'Jim? Jim Thorp?'

'Yes, it's me all right!'

'Praise the Lord, you're alive!'

He was relieved that she was pleased to see him. Craning his neck, he called up, 'Do you think you could either talk to me through a downstairs window or open the door? Otherwise I'm liable to get a permanent crick in my neck!'

She laughed, a most pleasant sound that he had quite forgotten. 'Yes, of course, I will be down momentarily.' She slammed the window shut.

By the time he got to the door again, she was opening it, her cheeks flushed with physical exertion and perhaps something else.

Having taken off his hat now, he held it nervously in front of him. He was glad he'd bothered to spruce himself up at Mrs McCall's. 'No need to run on my account, Anna. I can wait.'

'Well, that may be so.' Suddenly she grabbed his wrist and hauled him in over the threshold, slamming the door after him. 'But *I'm* done waiting, James Dexter Thorp!' Standing on tip-toe, she embraced him and planted a long and delightful kiss on his lips.

The images of several women in his past flitted through his mind and were instantly obliterated as he tasted her.

Abruptly remembering his reason for being here, he gripped her upper arms and gently eased her away from him. 'Whoa, Anna, let me get my breath!'

'Five years ago you couldn't get enough of my kisses!' she snapped, her grey-green eyes glaring.

'Is it really that long?' he asked, a glint in his eyes.

The lobby was small and intimate, lit by the yellow glow of a kerosene lamp.

Anna Comstock stood before him in her blue calico dress with its v-neckline hinting at a shadowy cleft that made his pulse race. She had celebrated her twenty-third birthday February last, he knew. When he'd last seen her she had been a precocious and beautiful girl on the cusp of womanhood. Now her generous curves told him she had entered that mystical realm and was comfortable there. He fleetingly recalled her firm bosom pressed against him moments before and regretted all the time lost. Her lips were full and pouting, still slightly moist after their contact with his.

'My, let me look at you! You've thickened out, Jim.' She fingered his scar. 'And you've definitely been in the wars.'

'Most of us have a scar or two to show for our efforts, Anna. A few have scars inside that don't show . . . ' He grinned. 'And let me look at you!'

Humouring him, she twirled slowly there in the lobby. Her raven black hair was swept back from her oval face and tied in a typical schoolmarm's bun. But nothing else about her was typical. Her cheeks were unblemished by sun, weather or premature ageing and possessed an attractive flush. Sparkling in the lambent light, her grey-green eyes were just as he remembered them, capable of being mischievous one second, angry the next.

She would have good cause to be angry tonight, he thought.

Suddenly breaking the mood, she hooked her arm in his. 'Come to the kitchen. We have a lot of catch-up to do. I imagine you could do with a coffee.'

Thorp swallowed as his stomach grumbled in protest but he refrained from declining. 'That would be swell, Anna.'

She led him along the short passage. A door on the left had a sign on it: Schoolroom. At the end they came into the back kitchen.

As she went over to the range, he sat at the rough wooden table and he glanced around. 'Nice place you have here. You made your dream happen, I see — the school and all.'

While she poured from the coffee-pot, she said, 'Yes, we got here in the spring of '63. It has been three long years of hard work, but I think I can safely say everything is working out just fine now.'

His heart sank but he went on, 'I've had some fulsome testimonials from the El Dorado's barkeep and Mrs McCall.'

Her cheeks glowed now. 'That's nice of you to say so.' She settled herself opposite him, the calico skirt swishing. 'So that means that you didn't come straight here to see me, did you?' She spooned some sugar into her cup and stirred meditatively. The sweetness had deserted her tone. 'Even after five years?'

'No.' Fingering his tight waistband, he hitched the gun-belt slightly and looked down at the hot coffee. 'Smells good.'

'You're supposed to drink the stuff, you know, not just smell it.'

He nodded and raised his head. He looked into her eyes and, his tone deep and husky, asked, 'Does Clyde live here with you these days?'

Her brow furrowed. 'No, he works out at the Maxwell ranch.' She added with a hint of pride, 'He's the foreman.'

She flushed again but now steel had entered her eyes and the tone in her voice chilled his bones. 'I am a fool. You didn't come to see me, did you? It's Clyde you want, is that it?'

Again he nodded and this time he sipped at the coffee; it scalded his throat, but he ignored the sharp discomfort as he really thought that he deserved that little amount of pain at least. Because that was nothing compared to the pain he was going to inflict on Anna.

Sure, she had a right to know, but how do you tell the only woman your heart had room for that you're here to kill her brother?

2

Within His Grasp

The last three years had flown by and Clyde Comstock had done very well for himself and he was real pleased that his kid sister was proud of him. And so she should be. He was foreman of the M-bar-W, no less! As he sat astride his piebald horse, watching the steers graze contentedly, he reflected that the best thing he ever did was move out of that no-hope town, Hope Springs. A dark shadow flitted across his mind but he shook it away.

If he had been given to introspection he might have pondered on the many dark shadows that plagued his thoughts and made his sleep restive. But he gave it no never mind. He lived for the moment and didn't dwell on the past. The past was done and gone, he reckoned. Consigned to the cesspit of history.

A rider was approaching and his pulse quickened as he recognized the man's build — Ike Douglas. His vest, chaps, roping cuffs and cartridge belt were all black leather.

'Hey, Ike, it's about time,' Clyde called. 'Have you hived them off yet?'

'Sure, boss.' A gold tooth glinted. 'I thought I'd take twelve from now on. Maxwell ain't gonna miss them anyways.'

Gritting his teeth, Clyde bit back a retort about not being paid to think. 'Fine, but don't take too many at once or one of the crew might suspect something. OK?'

'Sure, boss,' Ike Douglas said, mockingly fingering the brim of his hat. 'A dozen it is from now on in.' He whirled his horse round and headed to the western meadow.

Fuming inside, Clyde glanced over his shoulder. Slowly, he regained control of his rising temper as he spotted Abe and Ed two miles down range, busy discouraging a couple of mavericks from wandering off.

Ike was right, of course. Since his wife died, Joe Maxwell rarely ventured onto the range and stayed in his ranch house, content to keep company with his boring plain daughter Ellen. For over two years he had left the day-to-day running of the M-bar-W spread to his foreman. And now that Maxwell was ailing fast, Ellen and the ranch were up for grabs. So, sure, Ike was right, but he wasn't always right. He hadn't been right that time in the town of Deadfall three years back.

* * *

Ike Douglas, Jake Long and Will Hanson had been Clyde's pals for years. When they left schooling, which all of them had hated, they took on a succession of labouring jobs. Anything not to have to work for no pay on their home farms. Clyde's ma and pa didn't hold with him going around with those three, who they reckoned came from no-good families, but what the hell, he was old enough to do what he liked and one night he told them so.

His sister Anna and Ma were setting the table at that moment and rose to their feet, shock etched on their faces.

'For landsakes, son, have you taken leave of your senses?' Ma exclaimed.

Pa rose from his chair and instinctively reached for his thick leather belt. But Clyde snapped, 'No you don't, Pa, I'm too big for you now!' He lashed out with his fist, the blow glancing off his father's temple.

Stunned, Pa sank back in his chair.

Eyes brimming with tears, Ma ran over to Pa, all the while shrieking, 'Get out, get out! You ungrateful no-good!'

Clyde went. He didn't look back.

Ike's parents were happy enough to put him up. They were glad of an extra pair of hands to do the chores and, begrudgingly, Clyde obliged in payment for his keep. At least he no longer had to listen to Pa complaining about his laziness. The old man didn't understand. Clyde would work hard if the pay was worth it, though labouring for the town's carpenter didn't bring in that much.

Most evenings he and Ike rode into town, though they reckoned that Hope Springs was a sleepy place and could do with livening up. They regularly met Jake and Will at Coomb's Saloon, the only watering hole.

Everything changed on that Tuesday in January '63. They had the day off as they'd worked through the weekend in preparation for next week's founding festival. They were soon tanked up and got to joshing. They bemoaned the fact that they worked for a pittance and never had enough money to have a good time.

Will said, 'Let's rob a bank, just for the hell of it!'

'For the money, you mean, eh?' chuckled Jake.

Clyde glanced over his shoulder, but

nobody was paying them any attention. 'What, here in town?' he whispered.

'Hell, no!' laughed Jake. 'Me and Will got to talkin'. Spring Fork's a sleepy enough place. Most of the guns have gone to war. Only a few cowpokes left.'

'Should be easy enough,' Will said.

'Makes sense,' added Ike. 'No sense in messin' on our own doorstep.'

'Let's do it!' Clyde said, emboldened by the beer and the talk.

Downing the dregs of their drinks, they stepped outside. It was an odd feeling, Clyde thought, to feel this inebriated while the sun was still high. He joined in the laughter and mounted up.

Neighbouring Spring Fork was indeed just as quiet as their home town.

A cold clamminess trailed Clyde's spine and his hands were damp as he gripped the reins.

A couple of freight-wagons and a buckboard drove past. A few pedestrians crossed the street or strolled the boardwalk. Nobody had the slightest inkling about what was going to happen. That thought alone was exciting, Clyde reckoned as he pulled the brim of his hat down.

They pulled up their horses at the hitching rail and Ike reluctantly agreed to stay with the critters, holding their reins, for a quick getaway.

Three of them stepped loudly over the puncheon boards then stopped at the door of Stilson's Bank. Hastily, they pulled their bandannas up to cover the lower parts of their faces. Will withdrew his six-gun and opened the door to the bank. He walked inside and the other two followed.

'This is a hold up!' bawled Will, brandishing his weapon.

'Oh, dear Lord!' exclaimed a woman in black, a hand fluttering at her face as if she was going to faint.

'Everybody take it easy!' snapped Jake, 'and nobody'll get hurt!'

'Touch the ceiling, folks!' Will barked. The hands of tellers and customers went up.

Clyde dumped his saddlebag on the counter and ordered, 'Fill that with notes, fella.'

Eyes bulging, sweat beading his forehead, the teller shakily lowered his hands and turned to the safe behind him. He yanked the handle and opened it.

'No sudden moves!' warned Will.

It seemed much longer but it was only about a minute later when they were rushing out of the door and leaping onto their mounts. Ike swung up on his horse and, laughing and whooping, all four of them rode hell-for-leather out of town.

They took a roundabout route back and, before entering Hope Springs, they stopped in a dry arroyo and divvied up the money.

Will whistled. 'Hey, this is so easy!'

'Yeah, it beats all out of workin'!' exclaimed Jake.

'I reckon I'll get me a gold tooth!' laughed Ike. 'That tells folks I'm a man of substance!'

'What will you do with your money?' Jake asked Clyde.

'I think I'll save it. I want my own ranch, one day.'

'Dreamer!' said Will, giving Clyde a friendly punch on his arm.

Clyde felt so alive and excited by the whole experience. His heart was hammering fit to burst against his ribs. By God, this was even better than doing it with Betsy Marshall in the stable hay.

'If you're after gettin' a ranch, you'll need to rob a few more banks, my friend!' Ike advised.

'You mean we should do it again?' Clyde asked, realizing that he wanted to very much.

'You bet!' said Ike. 'But next time Will can hold the damned cayuses! I want to be in on the fun!'

Their next robbery was in the town of Deadfall and it wasn't fun at all. Things went badly wrong.

A bank teller made a sudden movement. Perhaps he was going for a hidden gun. Ike didn't stop to ask but shot him in the forehead.

Jake swore.

'Quick, get the hell out!' Clyde shouted, grabbing a half-full saddlebag.

Amid shrieks from the two women customers, Clyde ran for the door and Jake and Ike were close behind.

'What happened?' Will demanded as they hurriedly mounted their horses.

'The idiot teller got shot!' Clyde barked. 'Let's go afore the law's down on us!'

Clyde spurred his horse down the street. Ike was level with him and Jake and Will were close behind. Clyde could hear shouting and six-gun shots being fired behind them. Fear clenched his stomach as he glanced over his shoulder. Someone was aiming with a rifle, damn the bastard! He dug in his spurs.

He didn't see them until it was too late.

Both he and Ike rode down a woman and a young girl as they'd been hurrying across the street. A wicker basket and a prayer-book were flung in the air.

'Oh, Jesus!' Clyde moaned as he looked back again at the unmoving shapes in the rutted and puddle-pocked street.

At that moment, Clyde's bandanna slipped off and someone level with them on the boardwalk to the right exclaimed, 'Hey, you're Jed Comstock's kid!'

Ike fired his Dragoon Colt and two bullets hit the witness and the man fell back into a shop window amidst a spray of glass.

Nobody else had been near, nobody else had heard, Clyde thought as he replaced his bandanna.

He never remembered seeing the woman and child under his horse's hoofs. But he dreamed about mud-spattered broken bodies every night and woke in a stinking sweat.

If it hadn't been for Ike, I'd have had my neck stretched that day, Clyde thought and wheeled his piebald round to head back to the M-bar-W ranch house.

★   ★   ★

Ellen Maxwell was pacing up and down the veranda as Clyde rode under the timber arch with its M-bar-W shingle. She looked up as she heard his approach, her tanned, slightly chubby features twisted in anxiety. As he got closer he could see that her cheeks were mottled red; it was obvious that she had been crying.

He dismounted and tied the reins to the hitching post. 'Something wrong, Ellen?' he said softly, knowing the answer anyway. Still, it's polite to ask.

She came down the porch steps and grasped his muscular left arm, her blue-grey eyes showing concern. 'It's Pa, he's not too good. The stomach pains are awful and he can't keep no food down . . . '

'Have you sent for the doc?' He knew the answer to this question too. Joseph

Maxwell was a stubborn old coot and that was what Clyde was gambling on.

She shook her head. 'You know Pa, he won't see no sawbones. Says it's just old age, cramps!'

He removed his gloves and chucked her chin with a forefinger. His eyes bored into hers. 'Did you give him the laudanum?'

Ellen nodded and he could see hurt and fear in her eyes.

Good. He twisted his face with sincerity. 'But he's still in pain, is that it?'

'Yes.' Tears ran out of the corners of her pretty eyes. 'Much worse.'

Clyde sighed. His tone was gentle, not urgent, but forceful all the same. 'Well, honey, you've got to up the dose.'

She gasped at the thought.

'For the pain,' he firmly reminded her.

'But Doc Strang said I shouldn't; it might kill him . . . '

'OK, Ellen.' Clyde eased her hands off him and put a foot in the stirrup, ready to re-mount. 'I'll go into town, get the doc — '

'No!' Ellen grasped his hand and he felt a tremor run through her. 'Don't go,' she pleaded. 'I don't want to be alone, in case Pa . . . in case he . . . he . . . '

Clyde stepped down and turned back and crushed her to him. She smelled of carbolic; she'd probably been cleaning up after her old man. He brushed a length of auburn hair away from her forehead and kissed her there. 'Of course I'll stay, honey.'

They walked arm in arm up the steps and onto the stoop. 'If he's still in pain, he needs that laudanum,' he reminded her.

'Yes, you're right.' They entered the ranch house. 'I can't bear for him to be in so much pain.'

'Me neither, honey,' he whispered, taking off his hat and hanging it on an elkhorn rack by the door, as if making himself at home, he thought. He glimpsed his reflection in the mirror and couldn't resist slowing a pace to stroke his pencil-line moustache and short-cropped jet-black hair.

Joseph Maxwell was fifty-six but it seemed as if he had aged twenty years since Clyde last saw his boss yesterday. The man's normally sun-browned complexion was pallid, verging on jaundiced yellow. The lines in his face had deepened and multiplied. He opened deep-set eyes as he heard them both enter the bedroom.

'Glad I caught you, son,' Maxwell said in a croaking, weak voice. He held out a trembling hand, the fingertips now tinged a faint blue. His brown eyes seemed unfocused and were a dull muddy yellow now where once they had been bright and penetrating.

Clyde briefly shook the ailing man's hand and reassured him, 'The beef are doing fine, Mr Maxwell. They're real content on the meadow.'

Maxwell nodded then winced as pain suddenly stabbed his vitals.

Ellen rushed to the bedside table and

flustered over the bottle of laudanum. 'Oh, Pa!' she wailed.

Glancing briefly at his daughter, Maxwell croaked, 'Stop that caterwaulin', girl. You need to be strong.'

Hands trembling, she poured a measure into a pannikin and gently leaned over to touch his lips with it. 'Take this, Pa, it'll do you good.'

'What the hell, why not? It cain't do me no more harm now . . . '

That's what you reckon, Clyde thought, watching with just the right measure of concern on his face.

Maxwell sipped and then gulped the laudanum down. Then he turned his attention back to Clyde. 'You've been like a son to me these last few years . . . ' He wheezed. 'Since you took over from Hank Murphy, God rest his soul . . . '

'A sad day . . . ' he murmured, biting his lip. 'I'm just doing my job, Mr Maxwell.'

'Sure, son. But you're good at what you do.' He coughed and groaned and his clenched fist tapped his chest in annoyance. 'Well, I've talked with Ellen and she agrees it would be best if you and her got hitched. It's the best for the ranch.'

'Pa!' Ellen exclaimed and dropped the small metal cup on the floorboards.

Maxwell's brow wrinkled and he gazed vaguely in her direction. 'Well, we talked some about it, didn't we?'

'Yes, Pa, but to say it like that, out right there, it sounds, well, so . . . so . . . businesslike!'

Clyde grinned. 'I'd be honoured, sir. I know I'm only a hired hand, but I have a real great affection for Miss Ellen.'

'That's good,' rasped Maxwell. 'Good . . .' He closed his eyes and the lines etched on his face appeared to soften.

'The laudanum's working on his pain, honey,' Clyde whispered.

Ellen came round by his side and grasped his hand. She looked up at him, her eyes brimming with moisture. Her mouth twisted, possibly with a mixture of sadness and joy. 'You do want me, don't you, Clyde?'

'Sure, honey,' he said, smiling now.

'Pa and me, we haven't trapped you into anything, you know. You can up and leave, if you don't want to wed me. I will understand. Or you can stay on as foreman . . . Whatever you want, Clyde . . . '

Clyde pulled Ellen close and kissed her on the lips for the first time. At least that way it stopped her going on and on about him leaving. He had no intention of leaving now. Not when he had the ranch within his grasp.

3

A Reputation to Maintain

'Why didn't you write?' Anna asked, though it sounded more like an accusation.

'I did,' Thorp said. 'Well, I did for the first six months.' He shrugged. 'When I didn't get any letters from you, I kinda stopped . . . ' Sitting at her table, he nursed the coffee cup and gazed into the past, recalling the times he had hunkered in a sodden trench or behind a shell-splintered tree, scrawling a few words in those eerie quiet periods before all hell broke loose. 'Later, those times when I was fearful for my life at the next battle, I wrote you but I never mailed them.' He thumbed over his shoulder in the direction of the front of the building. 'They're in my saddlebags. Kinda kept them. Don't reckon I know why.'

Tears welled in Anna's eyes. 'But Jim, I didn't know where to write — had no address.'

She stood up and walked to the stove and brought back the coffee pot and refilled her cup. She faltered, noticing he'd hardly drunk his, but didn't comment. Returning the pot to the range, she stood with her back to him and fumbled in a skirt pocket.

Slowly, she turned, a hand clasped into a fist over her chest, clutching a white lace handkerchief. 'I thought you had been killed . . .'

Seeing the distress on her face, Thorp gritted his teeth. He would not say it but he now suspected that her brother Clyde had intercepted his letters and destroyed them. As much as he wanted to, he would not make Anna hate her brother. The war had built up enough hate for all eternity. 'The mail wasn't that reliable, so I hear,' he offered.

Anna came closer and he wanted to hold her but he sat very still. Waiting.

'But I cannot believe that all your

letters were lost, not every one. How many did you mail me?'

'About two dozen, I guess.'

A keen awareness entered her eyes as she stood looking down at him in his straight-backed chair. 'Clyde never liked you, did he?'

'Well, not since I stopped him bullying that kid with eyeglasses at the back of the schoolhouse.' He shook his head at the recollection. 'That was a humdinger of a fight, I can tell you.' He laughed, rubbing his chin. 'We ended up in the creek, got soaked. But Clyde never bullied anyone else in our class, that's for sure.'

She was twisting the handkerchief in her hands. 'Clyde didn't like you seeing me, either, did he?'

'No, I can't say as he did. But he couldn't do much about it, could he?'

She shook her head and turned away to face the back door, probably so he wouldn't see her tears. But he felt them, every one, because her shoulders shuddered as she tried to control her sobbing.

After about a minute, she faced him again, her eyes red-rimmed. 'But Clyde saw his chance when you went away, didn't he?'

Thorp stood up. She could condemn her brother, but he would not. 'I don't know for sure, Anna.'

'But I do. Clyde collected the mail. He would recognize your writing.' It was as if he wasn't there and she was thinking aloud. 'Oh, dear Lord, he must have destroyed your letters . . . ' She dabbed her eyes with the handkerchief. 'I never knew if you were alive or dead. He let me think you were dead.'

Right then Thorp wanted to feel his hands round Clyde's throat so he could crush the life out of him. Clyde didn't merit a clean death like his pals Jake Long and Will Hanson. 'That isn't the worst of it, Anna. That isn't really why I am here.'

'Are you some kind of lawman?'

'Sort of.' He left it at that and felt guilty at lying by omission.

She closed her eyes for a moment, as

if composing her response. Then she looked at him. 'Then I guess you know about the theft he was involved in.' It wasn't a question, more a statement.

He was surprised — and severely disappointed — that she knew. 'He told you?'

Anna nodded, thin-lipped. 'When he talked us into moving from Hope Springs, he said it was because of the new Enrolment Act.'

'I heard there were riots over that in New York.'

'Understandable, perhaps. Anyway, Clyde didn't want to be conscripted to go to war. But after a while, I got suspicious. We kept going from town to town for about six months. It was so unsettling. He seemed to be running from something or someone. I forced it out of him one night after he came back tipsy from the saloon. He told me everything.'

'But you were harbouring a fugitive, Anna. That's a mighty serious offence.'

'Oh, I dare say it is, Mr Sort-of-lawman. But he's my brother and it isn't as if anybody was hurt. He told me that he regretted what he'd done and promised that he was returning the stolen money a little at a time each month. Taking it out of his wage, he said. Anonymously, of course.'

'Of course. What theft are you talking about, by the way?'

'He and Will Hanson broke into Mr Goldberg's General Store and stole two-hundred dollars.' She folded her arms. 'By my reckoning, he should have repaid that last month. Now he's in the clear. So there's no need for you to hound him, is there?'

'If that were true, I'd be inclined to forgive and forget.'

'Of course it's true. Clyde wouldn't lie to me! He's my brother, for landsakes!'

'Is that the same brother you now suspect of tampering with the mail?'

She flushed. 'That was different. Yes, it was wrong.' She shook her head vigorously. 'Terribly wrong. But that does not signify. That was a personal, if misguided, act.'

'I have no wish to argue with you, Anna. In fact, I'm real pleased to see you again.' He absently touched his lips, remembering their kiss and now wished he hadn't brought it to a halt so soon.

'Likewise, I'm sure, Jim,' she admitted but her tone didn't sound as if she was in a kissable mood right now.

Thorp began, 'Four youths robbed a bank in Deadfall early in '63.'

'So?' she interrupted. 'We'd moved out of Hope Springs at about the same time, as I recall.'

He went on, 'Two of the varmints were Jake Long and Will Hanson.'

Anna gasped but said nothing. She stared, daring him to go on.

'For reasons I don't want to go into now, when I returned from the war I found out about it and spent quite a few months trying to track them down.'

'I don't see where this is leading, Jim, really I don't.' Her tone suggested she wanted to be finished with this.

Thorp persisted, however. 'Before

they died, Jake and Will told me who else was on that bank raid. They had no reason to lie.'

'You actually believe what those bandits said?' It was obvious to Thorp that she knew only too well where he was leading but she didn't want to go there.

When it came to the showdown, Jake had been bold but slow. It was a fair gunfight and Thorp got the drop on him. As Jake lay in the blood-smeared dusty street, he had asked, 'Why'd you come fer me?'

'I have my reasons. They're personal. Now Jake, you ain't got long. Do you want a priest afore you go?'

'Naw, I'm hell-bound for sure.' Jake coughed up bright red blood. 'It was good while it lasted, it's just ... I thought it'd last a mite longer, you know?'

'Tough deal, Jake. Now tell me, who was with you when you robbed the Deadfall bank?'

Jake laughed and it came out as a

gurgling sound. 'No point in keeping quiet,' he managed. 'They'll be joining me in hell soon enough, I warrant.' So he whispered three names and died messily.

Will Hanson had been a little harder to find but when he was accused in the saloon he didn't hesitate. He pulled out his two six-guns. He was fast but wide of accurate. Thorp received a flesh-wound in his left thigh and his two shells pounded into Will's chest, send-ing him crashing onto an abandoned faro table, scattering cards and money.

Lying on the beer-stained floor, gulping in vain at the musty air, Will listened as Thorp asked the same question he had put to his old pal Jake.

'You got Jake?' Will whispered plain-tively.

Thorp nodded. 'Tell me, Will. You never know, it may help when you get to stoke those fires. You may get time off of eternity if you tell me.'

Will giggled and gasped and Thorp reckoned he sounded like one of those witches out of that Macbeth play he'd seen back in Boston. 'OK, bounty hunter . . . I guess time off of eternity might sit pretty with me right now . . .' He mentioned two names.

Now Thorp stood up and faced Anna. 'I didn't want to tell you but you leave me no option.'

'Go on, then, say it!' she snapped, spots of red colouring both cheeks.

'They said that Ike Douglas and your Clyde were also in on it.'

'A bank raid?' she breathed, astonished. She sank down on her chair and put her head in a hand, staring at the wooden surface of the mahogany table. 'I don't believe it.'

'The bank teller, Blake Sturgess, was slain at the counter, Anna. Callously shot through the head. He had a wife and two sons, aged five and eight.'

Anna glanced up at him, eyes pleading for him to stop. He really didn't want to go on. But he felt compelled to strip away the lies that Clyde had told her. 'Two bystanders were trampled to death by their horses. I now know it was Ike and Clyde who rode them down.'

'You now know?' she echoed coldly. 'For God's sake, how do you know?'

'There were witnesses.'

'Witnesses?' The colour had drained from her face.

'In fact, one of them — Stan Hayes — was shot dead. We think Ike did that.'

'Excuse me,' she mumbled and stood up abruptly, tumbling her chair over as she hastened out the back door.

As he got up to set the chair right, he heard her expelling the contents of her stomach and he felt sick in his heart. He couldn't bring himself to sit down again and started pacing the kitchen floorboards.

Eventually, Anna returned and his heart tumbled. Her complexion was no better. Her mouth and chin shone wetly in the kerosene lamplight. She must have washed hastily at the pump outside.

'Accessory,' she said, 'isn't that what smart lawyers call it?'

Thorp nodded. 'Yes, it's possible Clyde is just an accessory,' he allowed in an even tone though he wanted to shout and pound his fist on the table. 'Except that there are the witnesses who saw him and Ike ride down those bystanders.'

This was not strictly true, he knew. The witnesses had identified the horses and the clothes and build of the men involved. And the two corpses he'd brought back for the bounty had tallied with the descriptions. It didn't take a schoolteacher to work out the identity of the remaining robbers still at large.

'Oh, dear Lord,' Anna moaned, 'this is unbearable.' She put her hands over her face for a few moments and he kept silent while she composed herself. Finally, she removed her hands and her red-rimmed, rather puffy, eyes studied him. 'What do you intend doing now?'

'I'll take Clyde in. Let the law take its course.'

'Clyde and Ike?'

'Yes,' Thorp said.

'Isn't that dangerous?'

'Sure, Anna. I can't say I like those odds, two on one. But they must face justice for what they've done. I can't walk away, even if it involves your brother.'

'Then I think you should leave my home right now, Jim Thorp, and get about your business!'

He nodded and turned for the entrance passage. 'Thanks for the coffee, Anna,' he said.

'Which you hardly touched,' she countered.

There was a dull ache in his chest as he picked up his hat from the table. 'Sorry, Anna. I'd already had my fill at Mrs McCall's.'

'Miss Comstock will do in future, sir. I have a reputation to maintain, after all.'

'Sure thing, Miss Comstock. I wouldn't want to sully the Comstock reputation.'

As soon as he said that he regretted it as the barb struck home. Anna faltered in her step for an instant, as if he had slapped her, then she glared at him.

He let it fall between them and moved towards the door. They walked along the short hall passage in silence. The atmosphere was thick enough to cut with the Bowie-knife at his belt.

Anna edged past him and opened the door. The same door she had shoved him against and delivered that memorable yet too brief kiss. He smiled grimly to himself. No chance of a farewell kiss now, he reckoned.

He stepped over the threshold and put on his hat. 'G'night, ma'am,' he said, and received no response. He descended the steps as the door slammed shut behind him.

It was strange and a little disconcerting to feel an unfamiliar band of tightness about his chest as he opened and closed the white gate and strode down the street to Mrs McCall's rooming house. Maybe this is what a breaking heart felt like, he mused. He didn't much care for it.

As he stood outside Widow McCall's, his step wavered. He was tempted to make the acquaintance of a soiled dove at the Bella Union bordello to take his mind off Anna Comstock. But it wasn't his mind he was concerned about, it was his damned heart.

4

Woman Trouble

Standing with her back up against the front door, Anna heard the glass pane rattle as she trembled with pent-up anger and frustration. 'Clyde, you utter fool!' she seethed, wringing her hands. She would never forgive him for depriving her of Jim's letters.

Get a grip, she told herself.

For God's sake, she owed her life to Clyde. But he had lied and lied about the theft. Ma and Pa would turn in their graves! The shame of it, to think that her brother was a bank robber. But he had saved her life. That doesn't make it right. People had died because of him. But he was her brother. Blood was thicker than water, surely?

As her mind tumbled and raged she was moving about the schoolhouse living quarters, blindly changing into a brown broadcloth skirt and a white cotton blouse, finally slipping on a pair of buckskin boots and a light leather jacket.

Now, she stood in front of the fly-blown bedroom mirror and was shocked at the image she presented. Her raven black hair was in disarray where it had come away from the bun. Her face was pallid, as if she was suffering from the ague, and her eyes were red-rimmed and puffed up.

She didn't care. She was ready to go out and that was all that mattered. It was obvious what she had to do. She must warn Clyde. She suspected he'd been led on by Ike Douglas. Whatever he had done — and she deplored his stupidity — she owed her brother that much.

Anna left the schoolhouse by the back door and when she got to the fence she hesitated, eyeing the buckboard resting on its shafts. Her chestnut horse was pacing in the small corral adjacent. She was fortunate — the animal was a gift from the town to enable her to take the children on nature outings. Still, she couldn't face a ride in the saddle tonight so, by the light of a lantern, she fixed the chestnut to the buckboard traces.

It was late but, she reflected, she had no choice.

At least the moon was full and she could see her way tolerably well. She geed up the chestnut and drove along the dusty track round the back of the eastern side of town, praying that nobody would see her. It looked as though most of the bedroom lights were out. The lights of the Bodines' house were still on and The Gem saloon, but that was all. Then the road curved in a sharp tree-lined bend away to the east and she lost her view of the town.

Before long she was bouncing on the sprung seat as the wheels met the rutted main road that led after five miles to the fork which in turn veered south-east to the Judd farm and south-west to the Maxwell ranch.

★ ★ ★

When Anna finally drove under the M-bar-W ranch house arch and pulled up outside the bunkhouse, she had no idea what the time was or how long she had taken to get there. But it was late, probably the early hours of the morning. She felt tired and bruised. Every bone in her body seemed to ache after the recklessly fast drive over the rough trail.

There were no lights on at the Maxwell ranch house or the bunk-house.

Draping the reins on the brake handle, Anna pressed her hands behind her to ease her lower back. After a moment, she stepped down. Tethering the reins to a post, she heard a dog on a chain barking stridently. The mutt had done its job, because after a moment, a ranch house light came on.

'Who is there?' Anna recognized the tremulous voice of Ellen Maxwell. Now she saw the rancher's daughter, silhouetted against the lit window and in one hand she carried a lantern. 'I have a shotgun. Identify yourself!'

'Ellen, it's me, Anna Comstock!' She walked quickly towards the veranda. 'I'm sorry to disturb you at this late hour.'

The gun clattered against the clapboard wall and the lantern bobbed closer with Ellen's footsteps. 'What's the matter?'

'I need to see Clyde. It is most urgent!'

'Are you all right?'

'Yes, I am, thank you. Just a mite distraught. But if I could speak with my brother, I'm sure everything will be all right.'

'Hey, sis, what's going on?' grumbled Clyde as he came out of the bunkhouse, the lit doorway behind him. He was buttoning up his green checked shirt, its tails dangling. The other men inside were grumbling loudly and colouring the night blue concerning the intrusive light and their disturbed sleep.

Anna grasped Ellen's hand. 'I'm sorry, but it won't take long. Can we go over there?' She pointed to the stables.

'Yes, of course, my dear. Take this.' She handed Anna the lantern.

'Thank you.'

Holding the lantern aloft, Anna walked over to the stables. Adjusting his shirt in his waistband, Clyde joined her.

They stopped by the stable door. Anna suspended the lantern on a hook and they were in a circle of flickering light.

Clyde gently grabbed her arm and whispered, 'What in tarnation are you doing out here, sis?'

'Jim Thorp's in town and he's looking for you.' All the way here she had planned to say so many things first, instead of this bald statement.

'Looking for me? You mean he's alive?'

'I know about the letters, Clyde,' she

said, her voice croaking a little.

He let go and took a pace back, arms out-spread in a gesture of honesty. 'He didn't care for you, Anna. Else why'd he go off to fight, eh?'

She balled up her hands into fists and shouted, 'He told me about your bank raid at Deadfall.'

Clyde put a finger to his mouth. 'Hey, not so loud! What is this — a bank raid? Me?' Anna took a pace forward and slapped him hard.

Her brother staggered back, a hand to his cheek. 'Hey, what'd you do that for?'

'You lied to me before and you're lying now! Can't you see this is serious?'

He chuckled. 'I might be chary of you, sis, you pack a mean slap, but I ain't afeared of no Jim Thorp.'

Now she was really riled and grabbed him by his shirt-front and tried to shake some sense into him. 'Get serious, Clyde! I think Jim has already killed Jake Long and Will Hanson!'

His jaw dropped. 'The bastard killed Jake and Will? What is he, some kinda lawman?'

'I suppose so . . . Something like that.'

'My God, Jake and Will . . . '

She held tightly to his shirt as if clutching at straws. 'If you give yourself up, plead you were an accessory . . . '

'Yeah, it was Jake and Will who got us to rob the first bank in Spring Fork.'

Anna abruptly let go of her brother's shirt. 'First bank? There was more than one?'

'Yeah. It was their fault — Will and Jake's.' He gestured vaguely. 'I just went along for the ride. It kinda seemed like fun.'

'Fun? For pity's sake, people died!'

He started pacing closer to the bunkhouse, a hand scratching his head. 'I need to think, sis. Need time.'

'You don't have any time! Jim Thorp will be here tomorrow, I'm sure of it. You have to get away. Run, Clyde.'

'Get away?' He laughed. 'Run? I can't

do that, sis. No way!'

'Jim Thorp knows you work here.'

Clyde laughed again, stridently. 'Work here?' He raised his voice now. 'Jesus, sis, I almost own the place! Me and Ellen, we're going to get hitched. We got her pa's blessing an' all!'

Anna stepped back in shock, as if she had been hit. This was a night for shocks, it seemed. She realized that she didn't know her brother at all.

Tears streaming, she turned on her heel and retraced her steps to the buckboard. 'Married? You?' She flung the words over her shoulder. 'Don't make me laugh! You only ever looked out for yourself, Clyde.' She raised a leg to clamber up. 'You don't care for anybody else. You don't love anyone but Clyde Comstock!'

He must have moved fast, because in the next instant Clyde was standing there beside her, grabbing her arm. He jerked her away from the wagon. 'I saved your hide, sis, and don't you forget it!'

Knuckling away tears, she said, her lips trembling on the words, 'Well, brother, I reckon we're now even!' She shrugged his hand off her arm and climbed up into the seat. She purposefully picked up the whip and glared.

'Yeah, OK,' he said, backing off and waving a placatory hand in the air. 'Go back to town. Thanks for the warning, sis.'

As she drove the wagon round in a semi-circle and steered back under the arch, Clyde cursed and stamped his boot in the dirt. 'Goddamn you, sis!' He stormed back to the bunkhouse. 'What she needs is a man to knock her into shape. She's too full of herself! If some man took her down a peg or two, maybe she wouldn't act as my dad-blamed conscience!'

'Clyde, is everything all right?'

He glanced up and saw Ellen patiently waiting on the ranch house stoop. He didn't want to face her tonight. Not now. He called, 'Just a little woman trouble, is all, Ellen! She'll be right as rain tomorrow!' He waved. 'Going to get shut-eye, we all have to be up early — sorry about the commotion!'

'OK, Clyde,' Ellen called back. 'See you tomorrow!' She picked up the shotgun and went inside.

As he stepped onto the boardwalk at the entrance to the bunkhouse, Clyde was met by two ranch-hands, Abe Dodds and Ed Nash. 'Sorry about the ruckus, fellas.' He forced a knowing chuckle. 'Sister trouble.'

'That's OK, boss,' Abe said.

Clyde noticed that they were dressed for riding. 'What gives? You ain't due out on the range for a good three hours yet.'

'Once we're awake,' Ed explained, 'we cain't get back to sleep nohow, boss. We thought we'd do you a favour and go out early, like.'

Clyde shrugged. 'If that's what you hanker after, go to it. I'll see if you can't have extra chow when you get back.' He slapped the clapboard wall and grinned. 'No extra pay, though.'

'Extra chow will be just fine, boss,' Abe said.

The two of them hastened to the stables to saddle up by the light of the lantern Anna had left.

'Keen bastards,' Clyde mused, shaking his head, and went inside the bunkhouse.

★　★　★

'D'you think this is such a good idea?' yawned Ed, as they rode at a brisk pace along the trail that headed back into town. He absently knuckled his thick red moustache; it matched his long curly ginger hair.

'Look, the boss wants his sister taught a lesson. We both heard him.' Abe's hat hung back on its chin-strap and his long mousey hair streamed behind him. 'Seeing as he's going to be the new owner mighty soon, it behoves us to get in his good books.'

'Behoves?' Ed laughed, his dark blue

eyes briefly glinting. 'Where'd you dig up a word like that, Abe?'

'I can talk just fine and dandy when I need to, Ed. Like when I get to teach the teacher a lesson, if you get my drift.'

'Oh, yeah, that's good. Teach the teacher. I like that. Seems to me we'll be doing Clyde a real big favour. You've gotta put sassy women in their place, my pa always said.'

'Exactly,' laughed Abe. 'And we get to have some fun while we're doing it. Can't lose, I reckon.'

Ed's forehead wrinkled in thought. 'What exactly are we going to do when we catch her?'

Abe chuckled. 'Just watch me, Ed. Then I'll let you do the same . . . '

Suddenly Ed exclaimed, 'There she is!'

A few dark purple clouds scudded away to reveal the clear moon which shed its light onto Anna Comstock driving her wagon along a section of track that led through a broad area of wheatgrass near a copse of spruce. The wheels sent dust into the moonlit night.

Now, wide awake at the prospect before them, the two men spurred on their horses.

★   ★   ★

The deathly stillness of the night was broken intermittently by crickets making an almighty racket. They seemed worse just here where there was a cluster of spruce and bushes. The critters were almost deafening, Anna thought. But not so loud that she couldn't hear the approaching horses. She glanced over her shoulder.

Two cowpokes were riding at a fair lick and closing on her wagon. The fork in the trail was about a mile ahead, so they had to be coming from the M-bar-W ranch. Maybe Clyde had forgotten something and had sent them to bring her back? She eased on the reins a moment. But why send two men with a message? Couldn't it wait till the morning?

Her throat constricted as some sixth sense told her that it would not be a good idea to let them catch up.

She gripped the reins tightly and cracked the whip over the head of her chestnut. The horse seemed to find additional energy and Anna felt the wagon jerk forward and move faster under her, the springs bouncing her all over the seat.

'Come on, girl!' she called to the horse. Never did give her a name.

Her black hair gusted in her eyes as she peered over her shoulder. Her heart lurched as she realized how close the riders were already. For pity's sake, what did they want?

One of them was coming up on her right, overtaking the wagon. He looked vaguely familiar, as if she had seen him in town or perhaps on the ranch when she'd visited Clyde, but she couldn't recollect a name. He grinned at her, his broken teeth surrounded by stubble. He had mousey hair, a bent nose and narrow eyes. 'Come on, Teach, pull up!'

he bawled. 'Let's you and me have some serious lessons!'

Anna's legs felt suddenly very weak. Now she knew what they wanted.

He leaned forward over the mane of his racing snorting horse and reached down to the traces of her buckboard.

She lashed out with her whip and he jerked back, swearing.

Laughter on her left caught her attention and she saw the other one, his curly ginger hair blowing in the breeze of their headlong ride.

Again she used the whip, this time on the gingerhaired cowpoke, and it broke skin across his pug nose. He eased his horse a mite as a hand went up to his nose. Heartened, she lashed out again, but now he grabbed the leather thong and tugged it out of her grasp.

In the same instant, while she had been intent on the ginger-haired man, the other one had grabbed the reins and was slowing down her horse.

The chestnut whinnied and the buckboard slowed and stopped.

Feeling suddenly helpless, she cast about her for a weapon, but she had none.

'Abe here's goin' to teach you a very serious lesson, Schoolmarm,' said the ginger-haired one, a hand rubbing the blood away from his lashed nose.

'Ed's right, ma'am.' Abe pointed at Ed's blood-striped nose. 'That's no way to treat your scholars!' he drawled.

'Scholars? I don't understand what you mean, sir.'

'You will! Now, don't just sit there!' Abe bawled. 'Get down off of there!'

'Off there,' she corrected. 'No need to say off of, you know . . .'

'Down, lady!' Abe growled.

There was a slight chance, she reasoned. Jump down, lose myself in the trees.

She held up her hands to mollify the bully. 'All right, all right, I'm getting down now,' she said, surprised at how steady her voice sounded.

Anna clambered down to the rutted earth of the track. Then, as the one called Abe dismounted, she darted to the right, keeping his horse between them, and ran over the hard rock-strewn terrain towards the copse of spruce.

'Hey, Ed, she's running off!' Abe called.

Ed swore.

Suddenly, a lariat looped over Anna's head and in seconds it tightened round her chest and the wind was pulled out of her as it was tautened. Roughly, the rope dragged her backwards and she almost lost her balance. She staggered, trying not to fall to the ground.

'Nice ropin', Ed!' Abe ran up to her.

Face suffused red with anger and lack of air, Anna felt Abe loosen the lariat from around her chest. She breathed in gratefully but she was alarmed to find that the loop was swiftly fastened round her neck. Her hands darted up to her throat but the rope was tugged tight and she found that she had to stumble back towards the wagon or choke, hauled by Ed from the commanding position on his horse.

In the meantime, Abe had tethered his horse to the back of the wagon. Now he removed leather horse hobbles from his saddlebag. He walked towards her and the look on his face sent her panting fearfully. Anna tried to back off but bumped into the solid form of Ed's horse. Ed jerked the lariat tighter, looping it round his saddle-horn, and she felt the rope digging into her neck and in seconds she was gasping for air. Feeling faint and dizzy, she waved her hands about, pleading, and the rope slackened a little.

She gulped in air.

'OK, lady, we'll do it the hard way.' Abe signed to Ed with the hobbles. 'Bring her round to the back of the buckboard.'

She struggled in vain as both men were over five feet six, weathered and strong and used to hogtying prime beef. She was as little trouble as a calf to their combined weight and muscle.

While Ed kept the lariat taut round

her throat, she dared not kick out or struggle; all he had to do was tug it just a little and she was choking. Maybe that would be for the best, she thought. Wasn't this what those writers called a fate worse than death? She felt tears pricking the corners of her eyes and she willed them away. She wouldn't give them the satisfaction of seeing her cry.

'Take it easy, Ed, she's goin' to be no fun if she's throttled.' Abe tied her wrists and ankles with the leather thongs to metal cleats at four corners of the bed of the buckboard. They both took great pleasure in manhandling her and at times she thought she was going to black out. Perhaps that would have been a mercy. But she stayed conscious and suffered the anger and shame of their pawing until she was tied spread-eagled on the buckboard floor.

At last, Ed removed the lariat from round her neck. She coughed and heaved on air with a mixture of relief and dread.

Abe stood astraddle her, a wicked-looking knife in his hand. 'Now, Schoolmarm, we aim to have us some biology lessons here.'

'You won't get away with this, Abe, or whatever your name is!'

'We're obeying instructions from our boss,' laughed Ed. 'That's what we're doing!'

'That's right, ma'am.' Leaning down, Abe grabbed her blouse and sliced it open with the knife. 'Seems to me, since you know my name, I can't afford to let you live.'

Anna gasped and pulled at the thongs in vain.

'I like 'em when they struggle,' Abe grinned and cut at her clothing again and again.

When he had finished, Abe gazed down at her and even in the moonlight she could see that his narrow hazel eyes were filled with lust. He sheathed his knife and hurriedly unfastened his gunbelt and hung it on the brake stick then quickly unbuckled his pants belt.

Anna squirmed as much as her tethers would allow.

'No need to act so eager, lady, we've got all night.'

'All night. Hell, I like that, Abe, I sure do!' Resting with both arms on the side of the buckboard, Ed was watching wide-eyed, grinning from ear to ear, saliva drooling down his chin.

'A night to remember so long as you live . . . ' promised Abe ominously in a thick aroused voice.

5

We All Have Regrets . . .

Abe's tone transformed abruptly and became a high-pitched shriek. From out of the night a thick coil of leather lashed round his neck, its tip tearing flesh from his cheek and forehead. While he clawed futilely at this almost living thing, he was pulled by his neck backwards. With his pants round his ankles, he lost his footing and fell off the buckboard, landing in a painful heap on the dirt trail.

'Abe?' said his sidekick Ed, dragging his eyes away from their victim.

A black blur met Ed's gaze and a leather-covered fist connected with his pug nose. Ed stumbled back and emitted a muffled scream. 'My dose, you boke my dose!'

'That isn't all I'm going to break!'

Thorp promised, slamming his boot-toe hard between Ed's legs. The man crumpled in agony on the ground.

From the buckboard Anna shouted, 'Jim!'

Too late. The bullwhip came over his head and he felt its stock press against his windpipe while Abe gripped both ends and thrust a knee into his back. Never underestimate an enemy. Abe had recovered faster than he would have thought possible; Thorp glimpsed Abe's discarded pants. If he didn't act soon, that garment might be the last thing he would see. The man was strong, which was to be expected.

Normal instinct when being throttled is to reach up with both hands to relieve the choking sensation. Thorp's hand dropped to his weapons-belt and unsheathed his Bowie-knife, flicked it round, caught it and back-stabbed where he knew Abe's supporting leg was likely to be.

It sank satisfyingly into thick thigh muscle and Abe immediately dropped the whip and stumbled backwards, cursing as he went.

Straightening up, Thorp massaged his throat with his silk bandanna and then used the material to wipe his Bowie-knife blade before sheathing it.

'Who the hell are you?' Abe demanded, sitting on his ass, hands clutching his bloody thigh.

'Your new teacher,' Thorp said, and crossed the ground between them in a blur. He delivered two swift kicks to Abe's chest and jaw and stamped down brutally hard between the man's legs.

Turning away, Thorp whistled for his horse and ran over to the buckboard.

'I'll cut you loose in a second, Anna.' His horse was by his side and he unfastened his bedroll and flung it over Anna. Then he clambered up and used his Bowie-knife to sever the leather thongs.

She held onto the blanket and trembled.

'I'll get you home now, Anna,' he said.

'Jim!'

'Don't bake no thudden move, mithter,' Ed said. He was tough, even with a broken nose. He had slunk up behind Thorp and shoved the barrel of his rifle into Thorp's back.

'You've got balls, I'll say that for you,' Thorp said.

'I ain't tho thure after what you done to me, mithter. I've a good mine to thoot you where you thtand!'

'What's stopping you?' Thorp enquired.

'Do it, man!' growled Abe, struggling to his feet. 'Kill the bastard!'

A loud click of a six-gun being cocked broke the tense tableau. 'You shoot him, I'll shoot you,' warned Anna. She was holding Abe's weapon, the holster still slung over the wagon's brake handle. 'Move back, Ed — and you, too, Abe — and we'll go our separate ways . . . all peaceable.'

'OK,' conceded Abe, since he stood there in his long johns and without a weapon.

Ed backed off towards his horse and

Abe followed him. In a few minutes they had managed to get into their saddles, though it was clear that sitting astride was painful. They both rode back the way they had come.

* * *

'I couldn't rest after talking with you,' Thorp explained as he sat beside Anna on the buckboard seat, gentling the reins.

Anna held the blanket tightly round her, her shoulders shaking with delayed shock. She was a plucky woman, he thought, as she listened.

'So I stopped for a while on Mrs McCall's stoop and then decided to turn back.' The chestnut led them to town while his sorrel was tethered to the rear and followed on. 'I was on my way to talk to you again when I saw you leave in the buggy.'

'I'm sorry, Jim, but I had to warn Clyde.' She shuddered, her eyes glistening. 'I hate him for what he has done, but I had to warn him.'

'I know,' Thorp said, 'a family thing. I managed to rouse Amos and got my horse saddled. I followed your trail and by the time I spotted you I guess you were on your way back from the M-bar-W. You seemed to be having a bit of trouble . . . Got there just in time, I reckon, Miss Comstock.'

She flushed. 'Anna will do, I think, after what you've seen tonight.'

'We shouldn't have let those two varmints go, Anna . . .'

'No, I suppose not, but I didn't want you getting shot on my account.'

He tipped his hat brim. 'Mighty considerate of you, ma'am.'

Despite her ordeal, she managed a smile. She put a hand on his. 'Jim, I don't really want anything about tonight to get out. Sheriff Latimer's a decent sort but he wouldn't be able to keep it quiet for long. In no time, it would be all round the town, with plenty of embellishments.'

'You're worried about your reputation, I guess,' he said, his tone tender.

'Yes, partly that, I think. But I want to continue working in this town. The children need me. Some gossips would ask why I was out on the trail at such an unearthly hour. A couple of harridans I could name but won't will suggest that I only got what I deserved! Then the parents would keep their children away . . . '

'Nice people you've got here in Bethesda.'

'Oh, they're mostly real fine. But we've got the usual bad-mouths that you'd get in any town.'

Thorp nodded. 'My instinct tells me to go see your Sheriff Latimer first thing in the morning and tell him about those two. If they thought they could get away with it with you, they might try it with another girl. And she might not be so lucky . . . '

Anna nodded. 'I hadn't thought about that. Maybe I should just tell Clyde — they must be his men, since they approached on the M-bar-W trail — and he will fire them.'

'OK, I'll keep quiet, Anna.'

When they got to the back of the schoolhouse, Thorp helped Anna down. She hugged his blanket to her.

'I'll look after your horse and wagon, Anna.'

'Thanks,' she croaked.

'Will you be all right — alone tonight?'

'Yes, thanks, Jim.' She forced a smile. 'I'll lock the door and come and see you tomorrow.'

He wanted to hug her but said, 'See you tomorrow, then.'

'Goodnight, Jim.'

She went inside and he started releasing the chestnut from its traces.

★ ★ ★

The floorboards creaked on the landing and Thorp was awake and holding his cocked six-gun when the knocking on the door started. Sounded like a gunbutt.

'I'm the sheriff, Mr Thorp. Have a

few questions for you!'

He wasn't surprised that the sheriff knew where he was; most small towns had a very efficient grapevine to pass on the details of any strangers. 'Can't it wait till the morning, Sheriff?'

'No it damned-well can't!' said another voice which Thorp instantly recognized.

'Clyde Comstock!' he called to the shut door. 'Long time, eh?'

'Mr Thorp!' the sheriff warned, 'I'm opening this door. Don't do anything rash.'

Thorp replaced his weapon in its holster. 'Come on in, Sheriff.' He had no intention of shooting it out with the law. Besides, he was curious to know what Clyde was up to.

Wearing his broadcloth trousers and socks, he was sitting up on the bed, his hair-covered chest bare, when the door opened.

Sheriff Henry Latimer was about fifty and tall, some six-five, with a sun-browned weathered complexion, grey hair and grey-blue eyes. His chin sported salt-and-pepper bristles and his badge was pinned to his leather vest.

Latimer's Colt .45 was aimed steadily at him but Thorp wasn't too concerned about that. He was chary of other weapons, though. Behind the sheriff stood Clyde and at his shoulder was Ed Nash, a bandage covering most of his nose and black specks of dried blood in his red moustache. Both of them wore guns but they kept them in their holsters.

'Dat's duh buthwhacker, Theriff!' Ed snarled nasally, peering round Clyde and pointing at Thorp.

'Bushwhack? Me?'

'Sheriff, I know him of old,' Clyde said. 'That's just the kind of trick he'd pull!'

Thorp thumbed at Ed. 'Why would I want to bushwhack this idiot?'

'Idiot!' exclaimed Ed. 'Theriff, you've gotta arretht him! He called me an idiot!'

'Easy now, Ed. Name-calling isn't an

offence in this territory just yet,' Latimer patiently observed over his shoulder.

'Sheriff,' Clyde insisted, 'there's no way one man could do so much damage to two of my best hands — unless he crept up on them!'

'He has a point, mister,' Latimer said to Thorp. 'Are you going to come quiet-like?'

'Sure, Sheriff. I'm certain it will all be sorted out tomorrow morning.' Thorp glanced wistfully down at his bed. 'I suppose the mattress in your cells isn't as comfortable, is it?'

Latimer shook his head. 'No, it isn't designed for comfort. Desperadoes don't deserve comfort.'

'Now I'm a desperado, am I?'

'Two witnesses say so, Mr Thorp. One of them's being patched up right now at Doc Strang's who don't take too kindly to being woken at this hour. But I'll leave that to the judge and jury.'

'Just give me a moment, will you?' Moving slowly so he would not give any itchy trigger fmgers the chance to twitch, Thorp slipped on his boots and unwound from the bed. He pulled his black shirt off the chair back and shrugged into it. As he buttoned it up, he eyed his belt draped over the bedpost.

'I'll look after your weapons, mister,' Latimer said, and slung Thorp's belt over his shoulder. He clicked a pair of handcuffs round Thorp's wrists, pinioning his hands in front of him. 'Let's be going, shall we?'

As their small group bustled down the stairs, Mrs Hiram McCall stood in the hallway, her eyes wide with concern. 'He seemed such a nice man, too,' she told the sheriff. 'Amos vouched for him and I've never known Amos be wrong about anyone before.'

'Sorry to disturb you, ma'am,' said Latimer and their group moved outside and closed the door behind them.

On the stoop of Mrs McCall's, Thorp glowered at Clyde. 'You haven't changed, Clyde, yet your sister can't see it.'

Clyde scowled. His response took time in coming. As they strolled past the telegraph office and Hayes Bank, Clyde finally said, 'I'll have you know, these days I'm a little older and wiser.'

Thorp nodded towards the bank. 'So you don't do them anymore, is that it?'

Even in the shadowy light of the boardwalk, Thorp could see that Clyde's face had darkened in anger. 'I don't know what you're talking about.'

Thorp shrugged. 'No matter, Clyde. Your past will be public knowledge when I get to trial.'

'*If* you get to trial . . . ' Clyde whispered, letting the implied threat linger.

They stepped down and crossed Main Street, heading towards the sheriff's office which was directly opposite the bank.

Pausing outside his office, Latimer turned to face Clyde and Ed. 'That's as far as you come tonight, folks.'

His tall gangling deputy came out to meet them. 'Sheriff. Everything OK?'

93

'Just fine, Jonas.' He eyed Clyde and Ed. 'Mr Thorp is my prisoner. I'll see you gentlemen in the morning when we can write up the charges.'

Clyde scowled and pulled Ed along with him and they sauntered away towards The Gem saloon. Its proprietor, Royce O'Keefe was a good friend of Clyde's.

'Afore we ride on back to the ranch, let's celebrate the bad guy getting caught!' Clyde shouted, clasping the shoulder of Ed as they stepped up to the batwings.

★ ★ ★

Sitting with his back against the jail's cool brick wall, Thorp watched Latimer write down a few notes in his log.

'Tell me, Sheriff, how does a bushwhacker manage to whip one man and knife another?' Thorp asked.

'That's got me a fair bit puzzled as well. My knowledge of bushwhackers is they shoot their targets in the back. If you're what they say, you aren't too good at it, are you? I mean, you left them alive!'

'We all have regrets in life, Sheriff . . . '

Latimer chuckled and leaned back in his chair. 'You know, if you don't tell me what went on between you fellers, I've got to go with the statements of those two M-bar-W hands.'

'Yes, I understand that. I have nothing to say tonight.'

'Well, Thorp, it's your funeral.'

'I should sincerely hope not, Sheriff.'

6

Just the Facts, Ma'Am.

'Why in tarnation won't you die?' Clyde growled at his bed-ridden boss. He leaned over, his face inches from Joseph Maxwell's. 'Die, damn you!'

Infuriatingly, there was still a faint glimmer of light behind those dull eyes. Stubborn intelligence.

It's your imagination, Clyde told himself, just the reflection from the oil-lamp which was turned down low on the bedside table.

Then the man's thin, cracked lips seemed to curve slightly, as if mocking Clyde.

Abruptly standing up, Clyde moved away and stood by the window. He peeled the curtain aside; the bunkhouse lights went out.

What had those idiots Ed and Abe

been up to earlier tonight? No matter, their story about being bushwhacked by Thorp suited his purpose. He and Ed had sunk a couple of whiskeys and then ridden back here. Ike had been awake and the three of them discussed going back into town tomorrow morning to press charges against Thorp.

While Ed went to bed to rest his aching body, Clyde and Ike leaned on the hitching rail and rolled and smoked their quirlies.

'He's always been a thorn in my side, Ike,' Clyde had moaned.

'Don't I know it,' agreed Ike, letting out smoke. 'You think he could cause trouble between you and Miss Ellen?'

Clyde scowled. He was really irritated by Thorp's stoic attitude even when arrested.

'I don't rightly know.' He threw the stub down and squashed it under his boot, putting more effort into that action than was required, as if he had wished that Thorp was there instead. 'See you tomorrow, Ike. I'm going in to check on old Maxwell.'

'OK, boss. See you in the mornin'.'

Now, Clyde glanced over his shoulder at his boss, who was after all his ticket to a future and a fortune. It was mighty tempting to smother Maxwell with his stained pillow. He bit his thumbnail, contemplating the act. No, it was too risky.

He turned and moved to the bedside and leaned forward again, eyeball to eyeball with the old man. 'Maybe I've been too subtle this time,' he said.

'Maybe I didn't put enough death cap in your laudanum.' He laughed, the sound bordering on hysteria, as he saw the terrible realization in the old man's eyes. 'You're too far gone to talk, old feller. I know, by God, because that's how it worked on my parents, see?'

Clyde stepped back and started pacing at the foot of the bed. After a few moments, he stopped in midstride, remembering how he had poisoned his family's well. He hadn't been thinking straight. Anna wasn't supposed to drink the poison too. He only wanted to get back at his parents for throwing him out. Not his sister, goddammit.

He used to sneak home about once a week to see Anna. She sometimes baked a pie for him, which he ate in one go. When he discovered that Anna had succumbed to the poison as well, he rode into town for the doctor and stayed by her bedside, nursing her, following the medic's instructions. Anna pulled through but their parents didn't; they took a week to die. He was quite the hero, saving his sister. If only they knew!

Moving to the bedside table, Clyde picked up the laudanum bottle. It was two-thirds empty. Pursing his lips, he removed the cap and lifted the bottle to the dying man's lips. 'Just a few more doses, boss, and you can join my damned parents!'

'Clyde, what are you doing?' Ellen's voice. She was standing in her white linen bed-shift at the bedroom doorway.

How long had she been there?

Clyde stood up and lowered the bottle to the table. 'Hello, honey. Your father was wanting a bit more pain-killer. He's in a bad way.' He scrutinized her chubby face, trying to glean from her expression whether or not she had heard anything.

What did I say? Did I threaten the old man or just think it? Did I think aloud?

'When did you get back? I didn't hear you.'

'Well, that isn't surprising, honey, you've been up all week nursing your pa. You're bound to be tired. I got back about ten minutes ago, I guess, and I was heading for the bunkhouse when I thought I'd check on your father.' He forced himself to stop. When he started constructing a tower of fabrication, he tended to talk on and on.

She brushed past Clyde, a fresh soap-scrubbed scent wafting from her. She didn't seem to care that she was naked beneath her shift, barely inches away from him. Until now, she'd been punctilious about the proprieties of behaviour between them. Perhaps it was concern for her father.

Ellen sat on the bed, took her father's hand in hers and held it to her lips. 'Oh, Pa, you ain't getting any better . . . ' Tears glistened on her cheeks.

Joseph Maxwell's eyes opened and moisture brimmed at the corners. His eyes moved hesitantly left and right, but his cracked lips only trembled ever so slightly. There was alarm and concern in his eyes but his daughter couldn't know that.

Clyde placed a hand on her shoulder and squeezed gently. Ellen closed her eyes and leaned her head against his midriff. He smiled down at his dying boss and the old man's eyes filled with tears.

'I think we should leave him to rest, honey,' Clyde said.

She nodded and he helped her up and they walked out of the door and turned right towards her bedroom.

★ ★ ★

'I've slept in better bedrooms,' Thorp said, stretching on the narrow bunk.

'I told you last night, mister, we don't go in for cosseting our felons.'

'Alleged felon, surely?'

'Are you always this picky when you wake up?'

Thorp chuckled. 'Is this our first argument, dear Sheriff? Just when we were getting along so well.'

Latimer groaned. 'I've got a feeling it's going to be a long day.'

Someone started banging on the office door.

'That's probably your breakfast.' Latimer unwound his frame and went to the door.

'Sheriff, you're spoiling me!' Thorp said.

Latimer's shoulders hunched but otherwise he ignored Thorp's banter. Unlocking the door, he let Jonas Johnson in, carrying a tray with two plates under metal covers.

'Mornin', Sheriff. Prisoner no trouble?'

Latimer relieved his deputy of the tray and put it down on his desk. 'He's been as docile as a rabbit, Jonas. Thanks for asking.'

'I'd've guarded him, if you'd said, Sheriff.'

'I know, son. I've just got a feeling about this one. I don't quite trust that Clyde Comstock.'

'Music to my ears!' chipped in Thorp.

Throwing his prisoner a scowl, Latimer said, 'Any sign of Comstock, by the way? I'm expecting him and Ed to formally press charges this morning.'

'No, but it's a mite early yet, Sheriff. I'll go and have a look around.'

'Yeah, and while you're at it, check with Doc Strang. I want to have a chat with him.'

'OK, Sheriff.' Jonas left.

'Are you waiting till the food's really cold before we get to eat it, Sheriff?' Thorp asked.

'By God, you can be a pain in the ass!' With that, Latimer picked up the cutlery and the covered plate and shoved them through the oblong opening in the bars. 'Maybe you'll stop being critical while you're eating. Though I doubt it!'

'Thanks, Sheriff.' Thorp lifted the cover and he was pleasantly surprised. Two eggs over easy, three bacon rashers, buttered bread and a mound of beans. 'It isn't often I get a free meal.'

'I had to fight the town committee to fund prisoners' meals, mister, so don't go mocking it!'

Pressing an egg between two slices of bread, Thorp said, 'Do innocent prisoners have to refund the cost of the meal?'

'Of course not!' Then he saw Thorp's smile. 'Oh, just eat your damned breakfast, damn you!'

* * *

'Breakfast in bed!' Clyde said, gently shaking Ellen's sheet-covered shoulder. His other hand balanced a tray of sausages, sweet taters and corn fritters and a mug of coffee. He was fully dressed, ready to go into town to press charges against Thorp.

Ellen sleepily brushed her eyes with a hand and suddenly everything from last night fell into place. Her eyes widened and she grabbed the edge of the sheet, sat up. Her lower lip trembled for a fraction of a second then she smiled as she recollected their passion.

He lowered the tray to her sheet-covered knees.

She sipped the coffee and pulled a face. 'I'll make us some fresh when I get up.'

'I don't have your knack at Java, honey.'

'No, but you're sure good at other things,' she purred, thoughtfully nudging a sausage with a forefinger, her eyes heavy-lidded. 'Will this become a habit?' she asked, cheeks dimpling. 'And I don't mean breakfast in bed.'

'I don't see why not — when we're married, of course.'

She picked up the sausage between

105

finger and thumb and bit into it. Grease drooled down her chin. 'I can go into town and see the preacher later today, if you like. Organise everything.'

He sat on the bed beside her. 'Sounds like a good idea to me, honey.'

'Why don't we do it again, right now?'

'But I'm dressed. And the food'll get cold.'

She peeled the sheet off her and said, 'I'm warm.'

He sighed. 'What the hell, it's only food!' He moved the tray to the dressing-table.

Clyde had to admit that she was a quick learner. He would have no regrets in that department after the marriage. A bonus, he reckoned.

Afterwards, he must have dozed off.

When Clyde woke up, he was still lying in bed, his clothes strewn over the floorboards.

But Ellen was standing in her night-shift on her side of the bed and tears welled in her eyes. Jeez, she was pointing the shotgun at him! Maybe she was having regrets about giving herself before the wedding?

'Ellen, what's wrong?' He sat up against the pillows and forced a grin. 'You know, honey, I said I'd marry you. There's no need for a shotgun.'

Tears streamed down her cheeks. She gulped and sighed but the weapon never wavered.

'Ellen, what's the matter?'

'Pa's dead, that's what's the matter!'

His first instinct was to get out of bed to show concern and, more importantly, to make sure.

As he pulled the sheet back to get up, she motioned threateningly with the gun barrel and barked, 'Move real slow, you swine, and get dressed!'

★　★　★

The office door opened and Anna walked in. She was dressed in a shining blue crinoline and a matching bonnet, tied with a ribbon. Quite fetching,

Thorp reckoned as he got to his feet. Her face was fixed in a purposeful expression; she didn't as much as look at him, but strode towards the sheriff.

Latimer unwound and stood up and offered his hand. 'Morning, ma'am.'

'Good morning, Sheriff.' Her tone was stern, her long hands pointedly remaining resting against her dress bodice.

'What can I do for you, Miss Comstock?'

'I've just been to Mrs McCall's and she told me what happened in the early hours of today. About you arresting Mr Thorp there.' She gestured at Thorp in the jail but didn't favour him even with a glance.

'I heard Thorp visited you last night, ma'am. An old friend, is he?'

'You shouldn't listen to gossip, Sheriff. I thought you dealt in facts.'

'Well, yes. Just the facts, ma'am.'

'And the facts are what, exactly?' She tapped a black laced-up boot impatiently.

'Well, two of your brother's cowpokes claim Thorp bushwhacked them on the trail last night. I'm waiting for Clyde to bring Ed Nash in to give me a signed statement so I can press charges. What's your interest, Miss Comstock?'

Thorp spoke out, 'I'm sure she's just being Christian and neighbourly, Sheriff.'

Anna gave him a steely glare that told him most firmly to keep quiet. Thorp held up two hands in surrender. Then she turned back to Latimer. 'Your Ed Nash and his nasty friend Abe Whoever attacked me on the trail last night, Sheriff. If it hadn't been for Mr Thorp rescuing me in the nick of time I fear they would have ravished and possibly even killed me.'

'Holy sh — er, sorry, ma'am.'

She glanced at Thorp, her lips pursed firmly, as if to say, 'There, I've said it!'

'You'd better take a seat.' Latimer pulled up a straight-backed chair by his desk.

'I'm not an invalid, Sheriff!'

'Sorry, I was just . . . '

'Just release Mr Thorp, will you?'

Latimer scratched the back of his head. 'Will you press charges, Miss Comstock? Against Abe Dodds and Ed Nash, I mean.'

'Is that the man's name? By God, yes, I will!'

'Well, in that case, I reckon I can release Mr Thorp.'

* * *

'Release your hand from the trigger, Ellen, so we can talk sensible about whatever has upset you.' Clyde finished pulling his boots on and stood up off the bed. 'Come on, honey.' He held out a placatory hand. Please.'

'Stop calling me 'honey'!' She backed to one side of the bedroom, away from the door. 'Go into Pa's room — but slow like or I'll blast you away.'

'OK, OK.' He moved to the door and turned left into old Maxwell's bedroom.

The first thing to hit him was the smell. Then he crossed the threshold and abruptly stopped in his tracks and stared.

The shotgun barrel jabbed into his back.

'Go on,' Ellen urged. 'Keep going!'

His heart was hammering as he saw the dead rancher sprawled across the bed. He couldn't see the laudanum bottle but there was an open drawer in the bedside table. Lying on the floorboards was a stubby pencil and five or six sheets of paper covered in the old man's handwriting.

Clyde wanted to speak but his mouth felt as dry as trail-dust.

'Pa wrote it all down afore he died,' Ellen said, her voice weary and cracked with grief. 'It's all there, Clyde. You poisoned him, just like you poisoned your parents!' She let out a heartbreaking sob and he felt the shotgun barrel stab into his back as she spoke every word. 'Dear Lord, I was going to marry you! Would you have poisoned me, once you had me and the ranch?'

His voice came out in a croak. 'Ellen, I don't know what your pa wrote. But it must've been the ramblings of a dying man, honest to God!'

'Honest to God?' she sobbed.

'Yes, honey. Look, that laudanum ain't poisoned. What d'you take me for?'

'What were you going to take me for, Clyde? Tell me that!' The barrel jabbed again.

Sweat ran down his spine. Nobody had the metal to face up to 00 buckshot, no matter who they were. Two cartridges, generously filled with nine balls each, made a hell of a lot of damage up close.

'Ellen, honey, can we leave your pa for a while. It ain't seemly shouting over his body like this.'

She sniffled and he sensed her wiping away her tears, probably with the sleeve of her night-shift. 'OK. Go into the kitchen, then. Slow-like.'

As soon as he entered the kitchen, he

knew she was going to call his bluff. In the middle of the large wooden table was the bottle of laudanum.

'OK, Clyde. You says it ain't poison. So drink it.'

He couldn't afford to hesitate, he realized, or she would know the truth for certain. He reached out and grasped the bottle, careful not to shake it.

Uncorking it, he raised the bottle towards his mouth. Then he turned to her and forced a grin. 'If I fall asleep on you while I'm standing here, honey, I hope you can catch me!'

She glared, not amused. 'Drink it!'

'Then what?'

'Then, Clyde, I might start to believe you.'

He nodded, steeling himself. What little death cap that remained in the concoction was likely lying at the bottom of the bottle as sediment. He took a sip.

'All of it!' she said, her voice breaking.

He took another gulp and out of the

corner of his eye he noticed Ellen's features softening, her brow wrinkling. Self-doubt was gnawing at her mind now. He dared to hope that all was not lost yet.

At that moment the kitchen door opened and he heard Ike call out in an exasperated voice, 'Hey, boss, we're ready to go into town!'

Then he saw Ike, standing with his hand on the door-handle.

Ike's mouth gaped at the sight of Ellen in her nightdress, framed in the internal doorway and backlit. His dark beady eyes registered the weapon and, in one swift action, he drew his Dragoon Colt and fired.

He was a good shot and the .44 slug hit Ellen's right shoulder. She shrieked and stumbled backwards. The shotgun went off, blasting to smithereens all of the wall-dresser's porcelain.

Ellen fell on her back on the floor and her weapon clattered across the boards.

7

I Want Them Alive.

'Oh no!' Clyde knelt beside Ellen. 'Ike, what've you done now?' His heart was pounding as his whole world started crumbling around his ears.

'Is that all the thanks I git?' Ike shouted, holstering his six-gun. 'Clyde, she was gonna shoot you!'

'Clyde,' Ellen whispered, her face twisted in pain, 'I saw you drink it . . . I believe you.'

'Hush, honey, don't talk now.' Grabbing a towel off the stove, Clyde covered the bloody wound and pressed firmly.

'Oh, Clyde, the pain . . . it hurts so. Give me some of that laudanum, dear.'

For a fraction of a second the temptation snaked into his mind. He shook his head. 'Nope, honey. Sorry.

The bottle broke when I dropped it,' he lied. 'Easy now.'

There was a smile on her lips as her eyes closed and she lost consciousness.

He said over his shoulder, 'Ike, you sure know how to get me into trouble!'

'Me, for Chrissakes? I told you, she had the drop on you!'

'Ike, just shut up arguing with me! Go tell Ed to get the buckboard ready. We're taking her to see Doc Strang. We can sort out the Thorp business afterwards, once Doc's patched her up.'

Ike shrugged and turned for the door. 'You're the boss.'

'Yeah, and while you're at it, give the rest of the ranch-hands the day off. Send them into town with an advance on their wages.' He was mindful of old Maxwell lying in the back, but he couldn't cope with that right now, not until Ellen was cared for and mending.

'Right, boss,' Ike said, and left.

For about ten minutes there was a whole lot of whooping and hollering as the hands saddled up and left, and then

116

Clyde lifted Ellen in his arms. He carried her out to the veranda just as Ed drew up with the buckboard. If he could keep her alive and pliant, the ranch could still be his. Nothing else mattered. He'd worked too hard to throw it all away. Ike was too damned trigger-happy; he decided that Ike would have to be sacrificed, perhaps on the way back from town.

* * *

With the town left in the relatively safe hands of Jonas, his deputy, Sheriff Latimer rode out with Anna and Thorp. It was a good day for making an arrest, Latimer opined. The sky was clear, the sun was shining and the town's schoolmarm rode alongside, bestowing on him her pretty smile from time to time. Thorp brought up the rear, as it seemed prudent that he shouldn't be the first to ride into the M-bar-W, considering the potential animosity the hands of that ranch might bear towards the stranger. They actually missed the M-bar-W hands by about ten minutes; Maxwell's men rode across country, rather than along the trail, making a beeline towards town to spend their early wages.

Anna pulled in her horse when they reached the trail near the copse of spruce where she had been attacked last night. A short distance on the right was a depression and a large cluster of boulders where the town's founders had fought off a redskin war-party.

Dismounting, Latimer checked over the marks on the trail. The buck-wagon tracks were evident, as were the places where a scuffle had occurred. He took off his hat and wiped its inner band. 'Beats me why Abe and Ed would do such a thing,' he said.

'Miss Comstock was alone and it was late,' suggested Thorp, his eyes on the trail ahead where dust was rising.

'But where were they going?' Latimer asked nobody in particular. 'They would be due out on the meadows in a couple of hours. And that's in the other direction. It's as if they set out from the Maxwell ranch expressly to attack you.' He shook his head. 'I don't get it. They ain't so bright, but I've never had any trouble from them over women afore.'

Anna's features turned pensive. 'I've just remembered. The one called Ed said they were obeying instructions from their boss ... Do they have a foreman?'

'Boss ... ' Latimer mused. He looked askance at Thorp. 'Are you suddenly thinking what I'm thinking?'

Thorp's eyes narrowed then he shook his head. 'No, Clyde's pretty low, but he wouldn't order his men to attack his sister.'

Anna paled.

'Anna, you must have heard wrong,' Thorp said.

She nodded, but shadows of doubt flickered across her eyes.

'You'd better mount up. We've got company.' Thorp whirled his horse around and moved off the trail.

A few hundred yards away a buckboard was approaching fast. As it got near, it was obvious that Clyde Comstock was driving. A horseman rode on either side — Ike Douglas and Ed Nash.

'Hold up there, Mr Comstock!' called Latimer, raising a hand.

The buckboard slithered to a halt and Clyde applied the brake. A cloud of dust briefly covered everyone.

Anna took a quick wary glance at Ed Nash, his nose criss-crossed by white medical tape, and looked away at her brother, her brow furrowing.

Thorp sat easily in the saddle, studying Ike through narrowed eyes.

'Hi, sis.' She nodded at him. 'What's the problem, Sheriff?' Clyde asked. 'I hope it won't take long, I've got to get to Doc Strang. It's urgent.' He thumbed behind. 'Miss Ellen was shot — a terrible accident.'

Thorp geed his sorrel forward to take a look.

Ellen Maxwell was lying on a cluster

of blankets and it was evident that she'd lost a fair amount of blood.

Cagey about going near Ed, Anna led her horse past Ike and dismounted and clambered onto the back of the buckboard.

'You OK, sis?' Clyde asked, the look on his face now curious. 'What're you doing out here with the sheriff, anyway?'

'It'll keep, Clyde,' she said, kneeling beside Ellen. 'Her bandage is too loose; it isn't doing its job.' She started undoing the blood-stained material.

For the first time Clyde noticed the presence of Thorp. 'What's he doing out of jail?'

'That's why I stopped you, Mr Comstock. I was on my way to the M-bar-W to arrest Ed Nash here. Looks like you've saved me a journey.'

Ed stared. 'Why me, Sheriff?' At least now his words were no longer nasal.

Clyde managed a laugh. 'But it's the word of two men against one.' He curled his lip. 'And Thorp ain't to be trusted.'

Ignoring the insult, Thorp kept his eyes on Ike.

'No, it ain't that simple,' Latimer said. 'Someone else is involved.'

Ed nervously eyed Anna but she didn't seem to be listening, as she was too engrossed in tightening the bandages.

'Who would that be, Sheriff?' Clyde peered over his shoulder at his sister re-tying Ellen's bandages. 'It doesn't signify, anyway. I need to get to the doc, *pronto*.'

Latimer backed his horse off the trail. 'You'd better get on, then. We'll talk later today, Mr Comstock.'

'Yes, I'd like to get to the bottom of whatever it is you're implying, Sheriff. Anyway, I won't be going anywhere until Ellen's out of danger.'

'No, I suppose not. We'll come along with you and I'll take Ed into custody when we get into town.'

Eyeing Anna in the buck-wagon, then Thorp, Ed panicked, but instead of wheeling his horse round to flee, he did the unexpected and leapt onto the back of the buckboard. He pulled out his six-gun but Thorp couldn't react because Anna was blocking his line of sight.

'I ain't going to jail, Sheriff!' Ed snarled.

Latimer had a better angle of view of Ed and was drawing his weapon when Ike shot him. The sheriff fell off his horse.

Thorp shot the Dragoon Colt out of Ike's hand.

Horses tried rearing in their traces while others whinnied.

'If you shoot any more, the school-teacher gets it!' snarled Ed, levelling his Navy Colt on Anna's temple.

'Ed?' Clyde exclaimed. 'What the hell?'

'I mean it, boss!' Ed snapped.

'Take it easy, Nash.' Thorp raised his weapon but wouldn't holster it.

Ed said, 'We're going back, Mr Comstock. I'm sorry, but we're going back!'

Swearing, Clyde released the brake and cracked his whip and the buckboard moved in a wide turn, back the way they'd come, with Anna still onboard.

Ike massaged his hand and gave Thorp a dark scowl. Wheeling his horse round, he followed the buckboard, trailing Ed's horse behind him.

'Go after them!' Latimer bawled as he struggled onto one knee. A dark blemish had appeared on his leather vest, just above his badge. Thorp hesitated. 'I'll be all right, dammit! Just go after them!'

Thorp nodded and swerved his mount round and gave chase. He pulled up his bandanna to cover his nose and mouth as he rode into the dust trailing from the wagon.

After a short while the buckboard hit a rock and lurched, its rear wheels leaving the ground for a few seconds. It was difficult to make them out through the clouds of dust, but it seemed that two standing figures on the bed of the buck-wagon collided together briefly then one of them fell off.

Drawing his six-gun, Thorp rode up to the still figure. As the dust cleared he saw it was Anna. He was sure his heart had stopped beating. He reined in and dismounted.

As he knelt beside her, she moved and turned over, choking on the dust. He let out a deep breath in gratitude.

'That damned Ike Douglas!' she said, coughing. 'Always led Clyde astray!'

Helping her to her feet, he said, 'Clyde's a grown man now, Anna. He only has himself to blame if he's in trouble.'

'You would say that, wouldn't you?' She coughed again.

He ran his hands over her arms and shoulders and she didn't seem to mind. 'You seem OK. Are you all right?'

'Yes. Just bruised some.' She agitatedly brushed down her skirts. 'Thanks.' She looked up into his eyes, her face smudged with dirt. 'Thanks for coming for me.'

He eyed the diminishing cloud of dust. He was torn in two. Take Anna back with the sheriff or go after Clyde and his sorry crew.

'I'll make it easy for you, Jim,' she said, as if reading his mind. 'I'm going with you to the M-bar-W.'

'When you look like that I know there's no point in arguing with you.' He swung into the saddle and offered Anna a hand. He yanked and hauled her up behind him, on top of his bedroll. 'It ain't going to be comfortable, Anna . . .'

'Just ride, Jim.'

He turned his horse round and they rode back to Latimer.

The sheriff stood holding the reins of two horses, Anna's and his own. 'I'm glad to see you're safe, Miss Comstock,' he said.

'You're hurt, Sheriff!' she exclaimed and jumped down.

'Just a flesh wound, ma'am.' Shielding his eyes against the sun, he peered up at Thorp. 'You going after them?'

'Yes. As soon as we get you on your horse.' Thorp dismounted and helped Latimer into his saddle. 'Can you take Miss Comstock back with you, Sheriff?'

Anna settled easily into her own saddle. 'Now just a minute, Jim. I said I was going with you!'

'You have students to teach. Besides which, this isn't a job for a woman.'

'As it happens, this is a holiday so my commitment to my pupils isn't in question — or any of your business.' She eyed him sternly and said, '*Besides*, I intend to see Clyde gets a fair trial and not a bullet for being a damnable nuisance.'

'Nuisance?' Thorp echoed, then let it drop when he remembered his own family and what he would do for them.

'Give in gracefully, Thorp.' The sheriff forced a chuckle past the pain barrier. 'She'll just wear you down.'

Thorp grinned as Anna pulled off her bonnet and dashed it to the ground. 'Are you ready, then?' she demanded.

'Will you be all right, Sheriff?' he asked.

'Yes. I'll send Jonas and Doc Strang out to the ranch. If you can, keep them pinned down there. For Miss Maxwell's sake.' He reached up and grabbed Thorp's arm. 'I want them alive.'

'I'll try, Sheriff, but that's a tall order.' He caught the earnest look on Anna's face. 'I'll do my best.'

'Well, that's all I can ask, Thorp.'

For about a minute they both watched the sheriff ride back to town.

Thorp slid a .36 shell into his revolver's empty chamber then put the weapon in its holster. 'Let's go, Anna.'

★ ★ ★

'The wagon's trail doesn't go to the ranch house,' Thorp observed, swinging back into the saddle. 'They're heading for Rapid Creek.' A single horse had broken off and gone in the direction of M-bar-W and he reckoned its tracks looked like they belonged to Ed Nash's critter.

'It figures,' she said. 'They have a

sawbones as well — Doc Wilson.'

He started riding along the buckboard ruts then stopped when he realized Anna wasn't following. He half-turned in the saddle. 'Is there a problem?'

'I think we should go to the ranch first, Jim.'

'Why?'

'Mr Maxwell needs to know what has happened. He might be worrying about his daughter.'

Thorp hesitated. Dammit, he was not used to being so indecisive. It was Anna's presence, she had a mighty strong effect on him. 'Every minute I delay . . . '

'I know, but we must check on Mr Maxwell.'

'Ed Nash left the trail, Anna. Headed for the M-bar-W.'

'That makes no never mind, Jim. I'm going to the ranch.' She geed her horse to the right.

He couldn't risk it. She might ride into a whole heap of trouble. The thought also occurred to him that she was attempting to give her brother more time to get away. Blood was supposed to be thicker than water, after all. But he wouldn't allow that thought to fester.

Reluctantly, he drew in alongside her. 'When we get there, keep well back. If there's any shooting, I don't want to have to worry about your safety.'

Anna went pale and nodded.

Later, they reined-in just in front of the M-bar-W shingle and entrance arch at the beginning of the short drive to the Maxwell ranch house, which was a single-storey frame building.

Nobody was about. To the left — on the west side of the property — were twelve thoroughbred horses standing in the corral that abutted onto the stables and livery building. No smoke issued from the kitchen chimney.

'It's a mite too quiet to my way of thinking,' Thorp said.

Although tall white-painted fencing partitioned the ranch house from the barn, bunkhouse and stables, from their vantage point on horseback Anna and Thorp could see beyond. The fence was expensive and substantial, separating the family from the men.

'This is a thriving ranch, Jim. Where are all the hands?'

Not a soul stirred near the bunkhouse and barn over on the right.

'Stay here. I'll go find out.'

'All right.'

He spurred his horse under the arch and hugged the animal's neck, offering as small a target as possible. He rode to the left, passing the corral, keeping an eye on the bunkhouse and the ranchhouse veranda. There was no sign of Nash's horse either at the hitching rail or in the corral. He approached at a tangent and finally dismounted at the entrance porch steps.

He pulled out his Remington sixgun. 'Anybody home?' he called, stepping onto the veranda.

The front door was ajar. Gingerly pushing it wide, he peered inside. Fine mahogany furniture, animal-fur rugs on the floor and walls, an aspidistra in a terracotta pot and everything neat and dandy. He stood quite still for several seconds to gauge his surroundings but he could detect no unusual sounds.

Thorp stepped back outside and waved to Anna to join him.

As Anna drew her horse up to the rail, a rifle shot rang out from the direction of the bunkhouse. She let out an involuntary shriek as it penetrated her flowing skirts and slapped hard into the saddle. She jumped down to the veranda steps as Thorp fanned his six-gun in the direction of the bunk-house roof, the blasts deafening to her ears.

'Get inside!' Thorp shouted, firing his second pistol.

She needed no urging. Lifting her skirts, Anna was already racing to the door and stumbled inside. Collapsing behind a winged armchair, she found that she was breathless and her heart was pounding.

Edging inside and reloading, Thorp said, 'That was close.'

'Don't say 'I told you so'.'

'I wouldn't dream of it,' he replied, but she wasn't paying attention.

Stooping low as she passed the windows, she moved to the back of the living room and entered the kitchen.

'Jim, it looks like there was a fight in here!'

Slamming the front door shut, Thorp crossed the room, crouching low. Another shot shattered a window and a picture above the dining-table on his left.

The kitchen floor was covered in broken porcelain and near the table was a dark patch — blood, he reckoned. He was surprised to find an uncorked bottle of laudanum under the table.

'What's that god-awful smell?' Anna asked.

'God knows. Maybe a dead cat. Take a look while I sneak out back,' he said, and swiftly exited from the kitchen door.

She felt very alone now that he had gone.

Feeling slightly foolish, she picked up a carving knife from the rack by the stove. Holding the weapon shakily in front of her, she walked to the interior door that led into a dark passage, which had two rooms leading off. From here the intermittent sounds of gunfire outside seemed distant, somewhere far away. As the door of the room at the end of the passage was open, she entered that one first. She stopped in shock and dropped the knife.

Her hand went up to her nose and mouth as she made out the corpse of Mr Maxwell.

★ ★ ★

The back door of the ranch house opened onto a small boarded porch which overlooked the yard. Directly opposite the door Thorp identified the privy and three large piles of logs covered by weathered tarpaulin; and to

134

the right, a kitchen garden. From here he could see most of the barn wall on his right. The bunkhouse was in front of that, almost level with the house. Stepping quietly across the dry earth, he moved to the east corner of the house and peered round.

A rifle barrel jutted over the ridge tiles of the bunkhouse roof. From the rooftop the gunman would have a clear view over the fence to the front veranda of the house.

There were two doors in the fence, one near this corner and one, he recalled, further along, level with the veranda. Because there was no more answering fire from the ranch house, the gunman would be getting anxious. Thorp raced to the door in the fence. From this acute angle he was concealed from the bunkhouse rooftop.

He unlatched the door and opened it. It didn't make a sound.

Thorp ran across the small open space between the fence and the barn.

As he ran he detected movement out

of the corner of his right eye. He dived down towards the barn wall as a fusillade of bullets rained down into the dry earth at his feet. Banging into the cottonwood planks at the side of the barn, he got to his feet and hurried round.

He saw Ed Nash standing on the sloping roof of the bunkhouse. He was easily recognizable with the nose plaster. He fired the rifle again but his footing wasn't too steady and the kick of the weapon upset his balance.

Taking advantage of the time that Nash spent regaining his equilibrium, Thorp dashed into the barn. Vital seconds passed while his eyes got accustomed to the subdued light inside. He headed for the ladder leading to the loft and its opening above the barn-doors. From this position, he was able to squint through a gap between the planks and see Nash cautiously placing one foot in front of another along the ridge of the bunkhouse roof, coming towards the northern end of the building, his worried eyes scanning the barn entrance.

Keeping to the shadows, Thorp walked over the straw and stood facing the centre of the loft opening: being in the shade, he wouldn't be visible to Nash.

Taking his time, he readied himself.

'Are you going to stay in hiding all day, Thorp?' Nash called. 'I've got a clear view from up here. After I git you I'm gonna settle with the teacher. She ain't goin' to testify agin me!'

It would be so much easier to shoot him where he stood, Thorp reckoned, then began his run up. The pounding sound of his booted feet was softened by the straw.

Thorp launched himself off the lip of the loft into thin air.

The distance between the barn and the bunkhouse was a little over six feet. The roof of the bunkhouse was about two feet lower than the loft opening.

By the time Nash realized what was happening it was too late to react. A black shape was diving out of the shadowy loft, directly towards him.

They collided and the pair of them crashed onto the sloping roof on the western side. A couple of tiles were dislodged.

Thorp landed on his feet, hard.

Nash wasn't so lucky; he hit the ground at an awkward angle and broke his ankle.

Lying next to Thorp, Nash screamed. 'My ankle! First my nose, now my ankle! You bastard!'

'The sheriff said he wants you alive but he didn't say anything about a few bruises and broken bones.' Thorp knocked him out with the butt of his revolver. 'Stops the moaning, anyway,' he mused, retrieving Nash's fallen rifle.

Then he stopped, seeing Anna sitting on the veranda steps, the sun glistening on her tears.

He ran up to her. 'What's happened? You're not hurt, are you?'

She didn't hear him, just kept staring at a few crumpled sheets of paper in her lap.

He stepped closer and his shadow covered her face. Startled, she looked up, the whites of her eyes shining through.

'Oh, it's you ... ' She sobbed and turned away. She wouldn't look at him as she said, 'You were right all along about Clyde.' Roughly brushing tears from her pale cheeks, Anna stared at her boots and handed him the sheets of paper.

8

Dry-Gulched

Thorp tied Ed Nash to the hitching rail in front of the house. He then wrote a brief note for Deputy Johnson to the effect that Mr Maxwell was found dead in his bed, Nash was responsible for attacking Anna, and they were now out tracking Clyde. He pinned the note to Nash's chest.

'Do you want to go on?' he asked Anna.

She nodded. 'Yes. It's more important than ever that we catch Clyde. He has many questions to answer. But I don't want to prevent Ellen Maxwell getting the medical help she needs.'

He bit his lip. Ellen Maxwell was a complication. But he agreed with Anna's sentiments. He'd face the problem soon enough, so no point in worrying about it now. 'OK. Let's ride,' he said, and mounted up.

As their journey progressed through tall grasses interspersed with blue-white beardtongue, Thorp found that he was again deeply stirred by Anna. She rode easy in the saddle and was a competent horsewoman. She was really knowledgeable about nature too, pointing out where he was likely to catch bobwhite quail and ring-necked pheasant. Her enthusiasm was infectious. 'You should be here in the spring,' she told Thorp. 'The meadows east of the town are a purple blaze of pasqueflower.'

He was pleased that she seemed to have blanked out what must have been a terrible shock. Clyde had always been impetuous, but to poison his own folks? It didn't make any kind of sense. He was careful to steer the conversation away from Clyde and her family so was happy enough to discuss the flora and fauna of her new home. She was keen about geography and her students enjoyed the subject.

On their approach, some minutes before they got there, they could hear the falls and their mounts whickered, sensing the water. Then there was a vague haze ahead and at Anna's urging they left the trail for a brief diversion.

When they topped the rise they could finally see the Bethesda waterfalls.

'Isn't it a wonderful sight?' she asked, turning to him in her saddle. Her face was alight, eyes shining. 'I never tire of seeing it!'

Thorp had to agree, it was impressive. Massive rocks had formed five natural arches and a series of waterfalls cascaded through them. The town's name derived from this spot. Several rainbows intercut. 'It's awesome,' he said.

'It's unique, really. The trail passes through the waterfall curtain,' she explained. 'It goes into a ravine which then develops into Corrigan Pass. And beyond is a quite lengthy trail through Sutter Canyon, leading to Rapid Creek and the Black Hills.'

'Quite a place,' he agreed. 'Let's get back to the trail.'

Thorp and Anna had to negotiate a gentle slope down to the trail which meandered up the side of the mountain towards the middle of the waterfall. On their way they disturbed the odd curlew and crane. Finally, when they were high up, the trail opened out and they could ride two abreast. Above were limber pine trees leaning at extreme angles, jutting into the clear blue sky.

* * *

'She looks too pale,' Clyde said, sitting next to the comatose Ellen. Behind them a waterfall roared. It provided an ideal, if deafening, screen to their hiding place in the cavern at the base of the falls. 'Why have we stopped here, anyway? Ellen needs a doc pretty bad.'

'I'm sorry, Clyde,' Ike said. 'I thought I saw dust behind us — maybe a posse. We can't hope to outrun them with a wagon.'

'I know, I know.'

'We can ambush them from here, though.' He lowered a hand on Clyde's shoulder. 'Then we can get on to Rapid Creek.'

With an effort Clyde pulled his attention away from Ellen. 'How's the hand, anyway?'

'Not too bad. Thorp's either a very good shot or a very lucky one. His slug barely grazed my knuckles.'

'Damn the man, he's good and lucky!' Clyde gazed down at Ellen's wan features. 'I was all set; my luck was changing for the good. If it hadn't been for Thorp turning up like that.'

'What was that about, in the kitchen?'

'A misunderstanding. She thought I was poisoning her old man.'

Ike laughed, showing rotting teeth.

'Why are you laughing?'

'Well, you dry-gulched foreman Hank Murphy for his job, so why wouldn't you poison her pa?'

'That was different, Ike, and you know it. Few of the crew liked Murphy.

He wasn't missed.'

Time and again, Ike had proved himself a useful friend. It was Ike's idea to make Murphy's death look like an accident.

Clyde had had an argument with the foreman while they were out on the range and they'd come to blows. He hadn't meant to hit him so hard with that rock, but once he started he couldn't stop. That was when Ike rode up and held him back.

As luck would have it, Ike had a stray calf slung over his saddle. 'Make it look like he lost his footing while chasing the dogie.'

So that's what they did. Carrying Murphy to a nearby ravine, they threw him down the scree slope and brained and flung the animal after him. They left Murphy's horse at the edge of the ravine, to be found by the search party next day.

Ike was full of good ideas. Even if sometimes he liked a little payback — small-time rustling Maxwell's beef, for example. 'I've seen you right, haven't I?' Clyde asked.

'That's as maybe. My point is, I'm just a mite concerned about my stash. If we run off now, I'm going to be out of pocket.'

'Stash? Didn't you put the money from the hived-off beef in a bank?'

'I don't trust banks, Clyde. You know, they get robbed.'

'Very funny. Anyway, we ain't running off. I told you, when the doc mends Ellen, we'll get wed and the ranch'll be mine!'

'Quiet,' Ike snapped. 'I think I heard horses!' He checked his rifle and slithered over the smooth boulders to the edge of the waterfall curtain.

★ ★ ★

Now, ahead of Thorp and Anna was a translucent water-pool, the rocks beneath the surface shimmering and clearly visible. At the lip of the pool, the water rushed down to another pool, before bursting raucously down into Clearwater Creek.

A single rifle shot shattered the tranquil water sounds.

Anna's horse reared up, blood splashing her face and bodice from the poor critter's clipped ear. She half fell, half jumped off the horse.

'That was close!' Thorp hastily dismounted and Anna was beside him in seconds. Pulling their horses with them, they scrabbled into concealment among boulders and quaking pine. A small bird let out a strident call of alarm, 'chika-dee-dee-dee'.

'Is Anna all right?' Clyde shouted above the din of crashing water.

'Yes,' Thorp called back, 'but no thanks to you!'

'That's just Ike, he's a bit troubled with an itchy trigger-finger!'

'Yeah, we saw the mess in the Maxwell kitchen!' Thorp replied. 'Clyde, we know all about Mr Maxwell!'

In response a bullet pinged against the boulders in front of them. And, surprisingly, another crashed through the trees behind them.

Thorp swore. 'What the hell?' They were trapped. Who the hell was the third gun?

'Let my sister out and she won't be harmed. But however you play it, Thorp, you're a gonner!'

Thorp turned to Anna. 'I can't get a bead on whoever's at our backs,' he explained.

'I'm not deserting you, Jim.'

Sombrely, he nodded. It was hours until darkness fell. 'We're going to be sitting ducks if we stay here.'

'Whatever you want to do, I'll agree to it.'

'Whatever?' he said, the corners of his mouth curving.

'Yes, Jim. Whatever.'

He kissed her and the taste of her was like last night, only better. After a while, he noticed a saltiness on his lips and he realized that she was crying.

★ ★ ★

Clyde gripped Ellen's limp wrist. The pulse was very faint but he was no sawbones. Anna had been as wan as this when she'd suffered from his poison. She'd pulled through, so there was hope for Ellen yet. A gunshot wound ain't like poison, though, he reminded himself.

'Who do you think that is behind Thorp?' Clyde asked.

'Don't know,' Ike replied, chuckling, 'but he's damned welcome.'

'Clyde!' Thorp called, voice echoing. 'Don't shoot! Your sister is coming out!'

Grinning, Clyde let go of Ellen's wrist and clambered off the buckboard. 'I've got him!' he said. Rushing to the edge of the waterfall curtain, he cupped his hands to his mouth and called out, 'All right! Let her come into the open!'

Ike readied his rifle.

A few seconds later they saw the blurred shape of Anna on her horse, riding into the water-pool.

'Wait till she's clear,' Clyde said, 'then give him hell!'

★ ★ ★

Cautiously, Anna eased Thorp's horse into the water-pool. It wasn't deep, the surface came up to the critter's haunches. Half-concealed under her draped skirts, Thorp hung onto a rope strap attached to the pommel while his heels were jammed into another loop tied to the cantle. He was on the side hidden from the waterfall cave; she only hoped that whoever was at their backs couldn't see him.

As their sorrel reached the lip of the pool, Anna's critter scented something, perhaps a garter snake, and whinnied and broke its leash. It plunged forward into view and into the pool.

Their sorrel whickered in response. Anna dug her heels in and the sorrel jumped, Jim's voice whispering calm words to it as they plunged over the edge.

Shots burst out above them. It was how she imagined it must have sounded during the conflict between the South and the North. Bullets whanged off rocks and thudded dully into tree trunks.

Her hair and skirts billowed upwards as they all fell. Her heart jumped, whether with exhilaration or fear she did not know.

Abruptly, their descent was harshly arrested as the sorrel's hoofs landed in the lower pool. Her buttocks and upper thighs jarred painfully as the saddle hit into her and she was winded, gulping for breath.

But the rocks beneath the sorrel's hoofs were slimy and slippery and before she could control the critter they tipped over the edge of this pool and plummeted amidst a down-soaring stream of spray that soaked her. Worse, she found it difficult to breathe, taking in chilly water that made her cough and spasm.

Their descent seemed to last an age but must have been mere seconds.

Shockingly cold and hard, the roiling base of the waterfalls engulfed them.

Here, it was very deep, where the water had pounded into the rock base for aeons. Even as she kicked herself free of the stirrups, her clothing threatened to drag her down. She was short of breath and terribly frightened because no matter how hard she tried to move her arms to pull herself up to the surface and blessed fresh air, she couldn't muster the strength. Her corset and bodice were tight, constricting, and her lungs were bursting.

9

Small Kernel of Humanity

'They've *both* gone over the falls!' Abe Dodds shouted as he broke cover and limped towards them. 'They tricked you, boss!'

Clyde ran through the cool invigorating waterfall and stared. 'Abe? What in tarnation are you doing here?'

'What about Thorp?' Ike demanded, his voice muffled by the waterfall.

'We'll check for his body in a moment.' For a fleeting instant he realized that they would also be checking for Anna's body. His sister. Inside, some remaining small kernel of humanity froze into a hard pebble; it lodged in his gut and threatened to trouble him, but he belched and felt immediately better.

Abe had reached him and they shook hands.

'The doc let me go back to the ranch.' He gestured down at his bandaged thigh. 'I'm supposed to rest.' He laughed. 'You can tell he learned his trade in the East — they're all soft out there!'

'But why are you here, Abe?' He clapped the man's shoulder. 'Mind you, I'm real pleased to see you!'

Ike emerged from the waterfall curtain. The only completely dry person was Abe Dodds.

'I was at the ranch resting in the bunkhouse when Ed got there . . . ' Abe explained.

'Where is he, by the way?' Ike asked.

'Tied up to a hitching rail with a note to the sheriff!'

'What?' Clyde barked.

Ike scowled. 'Ed was supposed to bring medical supplies from the ranch house. And food.'

'I know. He said so. Ed told me to saddle up — which is odd, since I usually tell him what to do — but he was keen to get away. He had his eye on some stash, he said.'

Ike growled, 'My stash!'

Clyde pressed a firm hand on Ike's shoulder. 'Calm down, friend. Abe's telling us about Ed.'

Abe shook his head. 'I told him I wasn't interested in any stash. We started arguing and then he noticed a couple of riders approaching the ranch. He told me to lie low. He'd deal with it, he said. I watched. I was tempted to help, but my leg still gives me gyp . . . '

'Was it Thorp?' Ike enquired.

'Yeah. And your sister, Mr Comstock. After they tied up Ed, they left. I reckoned they was set on following you, boss.'

'Why didn't you bring Ed with you?' Ike demanded.

'He had a broke ankle and was out cold. He wasn't going to be any use.'

Clyde clapped Abe on his shoulder. 'Well, it's good to have you here. Now, let's move. We have to get to Rapid Creek.'

'What about your sister?' Ike asked.

His eyes narrowing, Clyde said, 'My sister's gone. No good crying over that. I have to save Ellen so we can get things back to normal.'

'You ain't normal,' Ike whispered under his breath. He shrugged and said aloud, 'You're the boss.' Then he turned and barked, 'Abe, grab that horse they left.' Anna's critter was standing in the water-pool, drinking.

* * *

Thorp had let go of the rope strap as they hit the lower waterpool but his boot heels were still entangled in the cantle loop as his horse slipped over the edge. He banged his head on the rock lip and almost lost consciousness.

His headlong plunge into the cold waters at the base of the waterfall revived him and he quickly unsnagged his feet. Several olive green-brown shapes darted past him — walleye, distinctive with their spiny dorsal fins. Kicking hard, he swam up towards the light.

He broke surface at the same instant as Anna. Spluttering, she managed to say, 'I thought I was a gonner, then I started kicking real hard!'

Swimming across to her, he guided Anna to the edge and helped her climb onto a large smooth boulder. Water sluiced off her. He heaved himself out and sat regaining his breath beside her.

His sorrel was swimming towards him. He stood unsteadily, his boots full of water, and cautiously stepped over the jumble of wet rocks and pebbles to a shallow section. Gesturing to his horse, he waited patiently and finally grabbed the reins and helped the critter over the rocks to firm ground at the edge of a cluster of cottonwoods and willow.

Thorp unfastened the tarp and rain-slicker which were wrapped round his bedroll and spare clothes. He tossed a blanket across to Anna; only its edges were wet. 'Here, you can use this, if you want to get out of your wet things.'

'Thank you. But what about chasing Clyde and Ike?'

'I'd like to let them get a bit of a start first. That waterfall entrance to the pass is a sure-fire trap.' He unbuckled his weapons-belt and placed the pistols on a flat rock in readiness for cleaning. 'Our clothes have a fair chance of drying out on the rocks for an hour or so. Then we'll go on up again. Carefully.'

'That makes sense, I guess.' She turned and went behind a nearby bush.

While Anna divested herself of her clothes, Thorp peeled off his sodden shirt and sat down to remove his boots. Then he tugged at his wet trousers which clung awkwardly. Finally he was free of them. His big hands wrung most of the water out of the clothes. He felt the warmth from the sun on the soles of his feet as he lay the shirt above the trousers on a large flat boulder jutting into the river. He shrugged his torso out of the off-white long johns and let the sleeves dangle from his waist. The sun's warm rays felt good on his bare flesh.

Anna emerged from behind the bush,

158

holding out her clothing with one hand while the other retained the blanket edges to preserve her modesty. 'Can you lay them down for me?'

'Sure,' he said. He squeezed more water out of her clothes and put them next to his — pleated camisole above the pantaloons, the dress and corset alongside those.

The sun beat down, warming them. Birds chirruped and some frogs croaked downstream.

Anna appeared a mite self-conscious, standing there by the water's edge, draped in his blanket. She kept staring into space and her eyes were red-rimmed. He guessed that her thoughts were on her brother and those words written by old man Maxwell.

'Why don't you try to relax for a bit? Lie down and rest,' he suggested.

She gently flicked off her shoulder a water scorpion; even though it looked predatory, it wasn't harmful: a pupil had brought one to class in a jar. 'What will you do?'

It was sorely tempting to lie down with her. He grinned and knelt to pick up the Henry. 'I'll keep watch and check my weapon.'

'I pray you don't have to use it,' she said.

Chance would be a fine thing, he thought.

* * *

About an hour after Abe left the M-bar-W, a compact covered wagon pulled by two horses rode under the ranch shingle. Tom Durey was singing. Then he stopped. Normally, when he dropped by to trade liquor from his still for Miss Maxwell's pies, he heard unappreciative criticism from the ranch-hands, but now the place was unusually quiet.

Except for somebody suddenly shouting from the direction of the ranch house. 'What in tarnation?' Durey whispered. It was a cowpoke tied up to the hitching rail.

He braked the wagon a couple of feet away from Ed Nash. 'Where is everybody, Ed?'

'God knows, but hey, Tom, I'm sure glad to see you!'

Tom clambered down and stood there, arms folded, chuckling. 'What have they done to you, eh?' Then he spotted the note pinned to Ed's chest. He ripped it off. 'It says here you attacked the schoolmarm. The deputy's going to arrest you.' He glanced around. 'Must be due here soon, I reckon.'

'It's all lies, Tom, spread about by that swine Thorp!'

Durey growled and grabbed Ed's vest. 'What's that about Thorp?'

Ed told him and a black cloud shrouded Durey's features.

'Now, Tom, will you cut me loose?'

'You're a cripple, Ed.' Durey agitatedly rubbed the red-raw welt round his neck, a souvenir from Thorp. 'You're no good to me. I might just leave you for the deputy.'

'No, wait, I know where there's lots of money and stuff. I've seen it — Ike's stash! I'll share it with you, if you cut me loose!'

Grunting, Tom Durey withdrew his knife and held it to Ed's throat. 'That depends on you, Ed. Fifty-fifty seems about right to me. What about you?'

'That seems a mite unfair, Tom,' Ed croaked.

Durey's knife nicked a tiny piece of flesh. 'Do we have a deal, Ed?'

'Yes,' Ed managed, 'we have a deal.'

Durey savagely cut Ed's ropes.

'Thanks, Tom,' Ed gasped, and rubbed a hand over his moustache and mouth. He eyed the bit of blood on his fingers and made an effort to control a shudder. 'Can I have a drink of water?'

'I ain't your servant. Get it yourself!'

Ed gestured at his broken ankle. 'It'd be quicker if you got the water,' he said, hopping awkwardly to the wagon. 'Then we'll go make ourselves rich!'

'Oh, OK. But don't start using that ankle as an excuse to make me wait on you. I got my pride, you know?'

'Yeah, I know, Tom, and I heard that Thorp dented it real bad.'

Durey growled and Nash decided to keep quiet about Thorp for the time being.

* * *

Durey's wagon moved out towards the meadows so they missed the arrival of Deputy Johnson by about thirty minutes. Jonas Johnson and Doc Strang dismounted and tied their horses to the hitching rail recently vacated by Nash.

'Place is damned quiet, Doc, eh?'

Doc Strang harrumphed and held back while Jonas climbed the front steps, his revolver drawn.

'Looks like there was a heck of a lot of shooting going on here,' Jonas observed, indicating the bulletholes in the wood and the smashed windows. 'Stay there till I check out the house, Doc.'

'I intend to, Jonas, don't you worry.'

A few minutes later, after Jonas found the corpse of Mr Maxwell and the doctor pronounced him decidedly dead, they stepped out into the fresh air and sat on the stoop.

'It don't make any kind of sense,' Jonas mused, shaking his head. 'There's been too much traffic around here, so I can't tell what happened,' he added, gesturing at the churned-up ground around the hitching rail. 'What do you make of it, Doc?'

'I don't have a clue, Jonas.' Strang used a large white linen handkerchief to wipe his perspiring face. 'I came out to tend Miss Maxwell and she isn't here, so my duty is back in town with my patients. I'll tell Nils to come out and collect Mr Maxwell.' Nils Kolan was the town's carpenter and undertaker.

'I suppose it's possible that Clyde took Miss Ellen to Rapid Creek.'

'That's possible, Jonas. You follow them, if you want. But I'm going back to town.'

Jonas shook his head. 'No, Doc. I'll

go report to the sheriff, see what he reckons. I don't think he'd want me gallivanting off right now, what with him incapacitated and all.'

* * *

Anna was shaken awake by Thorp. 'What, how long did I sleep?'

'About an hour. Our clothes are dry, 'cepting our boots.'

While he dressed, she took her clothes behind Anna's Bush, walking unconcerned past a red-sided garter snake basking on a rock.

When Anna emerged ten minutes later, Thorp had mounted his sorrel and was waiting patiently.

He pointed to the camisole and corset still lying on a rock. 'Aren't you missing some garments, Miss Comstock?'

She gazed up at him, arms on her hips. 'I surely am, Mr Thorp. I'll be a mite more comfortable on the back of your horse without those things.' She scooped up the undergarments and stuffed them in his saddlebag.

'I hope nobody gets to search those bags. I'd have a lot of explaining to do!'

'You'd think of something, I'm sure,' she said, offering her hand.

He swung her up behind him. It was good to feel her arms wrapped around his waist.

'We'll take it easy,' he said. 'When we get to the ambush spot, I'll go on ahead and you bring up my horse when I give the all-clear.'

'Just be careful, Jim.'

That expression of concern sounded mighty nice, too, he thought as he set out on the winding trail.

They traversed the side of Grimm Mountain and eventually came out at the Five Arches, where they'd been ambushed a couple of hours earlier.

As planned, he dismounted and put on his rainslicker. 'No point in getting soaked again,' he said, 'though I have to admit you look real fine in wet clothes, Miss Comstock.'

Although she was blushing, she eyed him steadily and said, 'You too, I might add.'

He grinned then turned serious. 'Wait till I call you.'

Pistol cocked, Thorp edged towards the waterfall. There were no unusual sounds coming from anywhere in the vicinity. Determined not to enter the waterfall cavern along the trail, he clambered slowly up the left-hand scree and rocks. He stopped several times to listen but there was only the sound of the waterfall and passing birds. He moved to the left-hand side of the waterfall.

Pulling his hat tight over his forehead and shucking his collar up, he hurtled through the waterfall and entered the cavern, his pulse racing. Any second he expected to be shot.

Sinking down to one knee, he spat out water and eyed the rocks ahead.

Empty. Nobody.

There was a strong musty smell of bats but if they were there he couldn't see or hear them.

The shadows of the cleft in the mountainside signified the trail ahead.

He called out, 'Come on through, Anna. It's safe!'

Less than a minute later, Anna, covered in the tarp, rode into the water curtain.

He stepped forward and took the reins and led his horse along the trail, stopping from time to time to check sign.

Astride the sorrel, Anna asked, 'How far ahead do you think they are?'

'A little over an hour, I'd say. The buckboard's moving slowly, they don't want to lose a wheel on this rocky part of trail.'

'Maybe Clyde cares for Ellen,' Anna said. 'Maybe he has feelings for her and wants to get her patched up.'

'Maybe,' Thorp allowed. 'And maybe he hopes to wed her and get the Maxwell ranch to boot.'

Anna went silent and Thorp glanced up at her, regretting his comment. She was studying the pommel, deep in thought. Her silence irked him, he realized, and it wasn't just because he was deprived of the sound of her voice.

★ ★ ★

'Clyde, is that you?' Ellen's voice was faint but it was good to hear that she'd recovered consciousness. That was a good sign, wasn't it?

Clyde leaned back from the buckboard seat and whispered, 'Yes, honey. I'm right here with you. We're taking you to Rapid Creek to see the doc.'

'Oh, my God, I remember now . . . ' She pointed to Ike's back as he rode on ahead. 'Ike shot me!'

'Whoa, steady, honey, it was a mistake. He didn't mean to.'

'Why are we going to Rapid Creek? What's wrong with Doc Strang?'

'Doc Strang's been called away.' The lie came readily enough; they always did. 'He's real busy so we're going to Rapid Creek.'

'I ache real bad, Clyde. All this bumping up and down hurts so.'

This wasn't surprising, he thought, as only his seat had springs.

'Can't we stop for a while?' she pleaded.

He glanced anxiously at Ike's back. Prudence said to keep going. But if Ellen could rest awhile and regain her strength, then she might be more likely to recover. There was no danger from either the sheriff or Thorp now. Clyde began to hope again. He halted the buckboard and applied the brake; Anna's horse, tied to the back, whickered.

Ahead, Ike's horse stopped and turned. 'What's the problem, Clyde?' Ike demanded.

'We need to rest up a bit. Ellen's come to. She needs to rest.'

Ike pursed his lips and clearly bit back whatever retort he was considering. 'Very well. You're the boss.'

'So you keep reminding me,' Clyde said. He gestured to clumps of tumbleweed and the odd dried-up tree. 'There's plenty of firewood here. We can have us some coffee.'

'While you play at domestic bliss, I'll go on ahead, make sure it's all clear for the wagon,' Ike said. 'Abe can check our back-trail. Just to be sure.'

'That's a good idea,' Clyde said.

'Yeah, I'm full of them.' He harshly tugged his horse round and cantered ahead while Abe rode back the way they had come.

★　★　★

Anna's spirits seemed to lift once they emerged from the shadowy gully. This canyon was wide enough so that they were again bathed in strong sunlight. Steam rose from the sorrel's flanks and the tarp bedroll.

Anna dismounted and glanced around at the two high canyon walls on either side of the wide trail. A pair of turkey vultures circled above.

Thorp wiped his horse down and

then tightened the girth. 'Ready for the final push?' he asked.

She nodded then looked him straight in the eyes. 'I know what I said before, Jim, but don't take any chances with your life on account of your promise.'

He pushed his hat back and smiled. 'I'll be careful, don't worry.' In one smooth movement he stepped into the stirrup, swung into the saddle and offered her his hand. She took it and was lifted onto the bedroll as if her weight was negligible.

'When I reckon we're about fifteen minutes off, I'll lower you down. Hide among the rocks until I get back.'

He felt her grip tighten on his waist. 'Yes,' she croaked, and he sensed that she was crying again.

Then she said, 'I did some thinking back there in the gulley. Clyde didn't post any money back to the storekeeper, did he?'

'Nope.'

'I don't suppose he robbed the storekeeper, did he?'

'Just banks. Always a liar, your Clyde.'

He felt her grip tense against him, then she softened. 'He never liked you.'

Thorp sighed. 'Nor me him, if hurtful truth be told.'

'At one time, Jim, that truth would have hurt me. But not now. You tolerated him to see me, didn't you?'

'Yes.' He scrutinized the trail. 'It was worth it, Anna.'

Reining-in, he said, 'This is where you get off.'

Standing there, looking up at him, she said, 'Be careful, Jim.'

He touched his hat brim. 'That's how I got through the war, Anna, by being careful. See you later.' He nodded and rode on, leaving her alone.

* ★ *

Abe had heard them talking, their voices bouncing off the rocks at this part of the canyon. He couldn't make out the words, only that it was a man and a woman. Had to be Thorp and the teacher. Lucky devils must have survived the drop, after all.

He hastily dismounted and, limping awkwardly, he pulled his horse behind a number of large boulders. Muffling the animal's nostrils with his bandanna, he waited, his rifle ready.

Sure enough, Thorp rode into view. The man was alone. He was intent on the trail ahead, nothing else.

It was tempting to take a potshot, but Thorp's horse moved fast, almost a blur. Besides, Abe wasn't that good a shot. He had a much better idea.

As the sound of Thorp's sorrel diminished, Abe left his horse and skulked back along the trail, sticking to the shadows.

He hadn't travelled more than a few hundred feet when he saw her, sitting on a rock. Even though she was bedraggled and dusty, she was a fair sight. Fair game, in fact.

He limped out of the shadows and waved the rifle at her. 'Congratulations on surviving the drop, Miss Comstock.'

She stood up, her mouth twisting in disdain. 'You can't threaten me, Abe Dodds. Clyde wouldn't take kindly to it!'

Abe spat into the dust. 'Your brother's losing his mind. As far as he's concerned, you're dead.'

10

Not Worth Dying For

Anna gasped and took a step back, realizing what Abe was implying. Her mouth was dry but it wasn't due to the heat. Her legs felt weak and she remembered the last time this man had power over her. Good God, was it only yesterday? She'd woken up half a dozen times during the night, covered in sweat, Dodds and Nash filling her nightmares with twisted, leering mouths and dark lustful eyes. Now the nightmare was in front of her.

She fumbled inside her dress pocket. 'I'd have thought you learned your lesson last night,' she said.

'Oh, it's lessons is it, schoolmarm?' He scowled and limped another step closer. 'I've got a damned limp because of you! I'll show you lessons!'

176

The handgun was nearly fourteen inches long and its barrel caught on the fabric. She tugged frantically. Before he got too near, she managed to pull out the revolver Jim had left with her — 'just in case', he'd said.

She cocked the hammer back and held the gun in both hands, pointing it at him. 'Don't come a step closer, or I'll shoot!'

Abe Dodds laughed disconcertingly. 'You're a game hussy!' In a swift blur of motion, he swung his rifle round and its walnut stock smashed into her hands. The pistol spun out of her grasp but didn't go off. Anna stumbled back into a hard boulder.

'Now, about those lessons, ma'am . . .'

★　★　★

'I've learned my lesson, Ellen,' Clyde said, cradling her head in his arms and offering her another sip of his coffee. 'Ike's been leading me astray for years. But since I met you and your pa, I've been a changed man, honey.'

She screwed up her face. 'Your coffee hasn't changed over the years, though — you can still float a horseshoe in it!' She laughed and then winced. Her face went white.

His hands trembling, he lowered her head against the blankets on the bed of the buckboard. 'I reckon we need to get going, honey. You've rested some, let's hope it's enough.'

She nodded. 'Thank you, Clyde. You've been good to me.' She closed her eyes. 'Really.'

He stared down at her pale yet rather serene face and caught his breath. Rather than giving her recuperative rest, this delay might be fatal, he thought. If she died, what happened to the ranch? He hadn't heard of any relatives back East — or anywhere else, come to that. She mustn't die, he told himself, clambering over to the buckboard seat. He grabbed the reins and pulled the brake free.

At least the horses were rested and

they were soon into their stride.

The buck-wagon bounced over the rocky trail. Clyde kept glancing over his shoulder at Ellen then further down the trail. Where the hell was Abe? And why wasn't Ike back yet? It was all Ike's fault anyway, just like he'd told Ellen. Ike had done the killing. Well, most of it. Damn him to hell!

★ ★ ★

Abe used the snout of his rifle to lift the edge of Anna's dress, revealing her pantaloons. He snarled, 'Take them things off!'

Anna gritted her teeth and shook her head.

'If you're good to me, I might let you live,' he wheedled, running the barrel up over her heaving bodice.

'Go to hell!' she snapped.

'Now that ain't very schoolmarmish, is it?' He swung the stock of the weapon into her stomach and she doubled up and sank to her knees.

With his free hand, he grabbed her hair and thrust her head back. He leaned forward and rasped his cheek against hers and gave her a hard, slobbering kiss. 'You taste and smell real nice, nicer than them painted cats at the Bella Union. Now just learn to do as I want!'

Anna gulped in air and sobbed, 'I'd rather die!'

'You don't really want to die,' he said, slapping her face. He grabbed the top of her bodice. 'It ain't worth dying for, you know?'

'You should've realized that before molesting the lady,' said Thorp, astride his sorrel. Neither Abe nor Anna had heard Thorp's approach; they'd been too involved in their own drama.

Abe thrust Anna away and whirled round, raising his rifle, levering a shell into the breech. Too slow, too late.

Thorp's revolver barked, shattering Abe's knee, the furthest from Anna. Shrieking in pain, Abe tumbled forward as his leg gave way under him. 'My blasted leg again!' Cursing, he rolled and fired the rifle blindly in Thorp's direction.

But Thorp seemed oblivious of the wild shots and rode purposefully towards the rolling figure of Abe.

Thorp fired twice and Abe lay quite still.

When he got to her, Thorp dismounted. Anna was kneeling against a boulder, catching her breath. Her eyes were filled with tears and she was shaking. 'That's twice you've saved me from that awful man,' she said.

He gently took her arms and helped her stand up. 'I can assure you that there won't be a third time.'

Sombrely, she brushed dust off her skirts and eyed the corpse. 'No, I guess not.' She cocked her head to one side, puzzlement on her features. 'You came back for me. Why?'

'Maybe I've acquired the habit of saving you from no-good cowpokes.'

'Seriously, Jim. You haven't been gone that long, you can't have caught up with Clyde, surely?'

'No. I *was* catching up, but I noticed the fresh tracks of a horse heading back along the trail. I reckoned that somebody had doubled back and I must have missed them. I rode as quickly as I could.'

She took his hand. 'Thank God you did.'

'Let's scout around,' he said, not letting go of her hand. 'I reckon Abe's horse is close by, and he won't be needing it.'

* * *

The trail wound down gradually from the mountains and about a mile ahead was the small township of Rapid Creek. From the mountains the river meandered in a zigzag course to the eastern side of the town, swelling at a series of rapids that debouched into a lake.

'We're nearly there!' Clyde called over his shoulder, but there was no response. He shook the reins and urged the horses on for the final leg.

It was a complete mystery about Ike. Had he gone back for his stash?

Possible, Clyde thought. Yet if Ike had believed that Ellen would pull through and marry me, he must have reckoned that he'd gain too. He wasn't to know that I consider him a liability.

Clyde shrugged. If Ike wanted to get out of my life, he thought, so be it. I have a ranch to run — and a past to hide! Laughing at the new freedom that Ike's absence presented, he lashed the reins and hurried the buckboard into town.

He'd been here several times before, once with Ike to check on the security of the bank, but that was a couple of weeks before he'd landed the job at the M-bar-W. Then, everything had changed. He'd become foreman and was promised to the owner's daughter. Certain aspects of his recent past were a bit hazy now, but he wasn't concerned.

He drew in the team outside Doctor

183

Wilson's. A few passers-by stared, curiosity piqued by his hasty arrival.

Clyde jumped down and ran round the buckboard and lifted Ellen into his arms. God, she was light. To think they'd woken this morning in her bed.

At that moment, Doctor Wilson stepped out of the surgery. He was a middle-aged man, in his shirt-sleeves, and wore a vest that sported a chain and fob watch. 'I saw you arrive in great haste, young man. Is the lady ill?'

'She's been shot, Doc!'

'Good heavens. You'd better bring her in — quickly man!' The doctor held the door open and followed Clyde in.

'Nurse, prepare the surgery at once,' the doctor hollered. 'Bullet wound!'

Clyde laid Ellen down on the darkly stained table. Those stains alarmed him. He glanced around at the shelves of books and the trolley holding strange metal instruments. The cupboard was filled with colourful bottles of scientific and weird nostrums and he idly wondered if death cap was among them.

'Can you save her, Doc?' Clyde asked, wringing his hands.

'Leave it to me, son.' As an aside he said, 'I'm afraid she has lost a lot of blood . . . '

'Just save her, Doc. Please!'

'I'll do the best I can. Now leave me to it, will you?'

'Come with me, sir.' The nurse, dressed in grey gingham with a white starched apron, gently led him out of the surgery and he sat down heavily in a deep brown leather chesterfield chair in the vestibule.

Clyde Comstock lowered his head into his hands and for the first time in many years he prayed. And, oddly, he didn't seek divine intervention for himself. He prayed that Ellen Maxwell would live.

★　★　★

Tom Durey's small covered wagon stood stationary on a slope of the meadow, the horses idly grazing. To the west was the M-bar-W herd of cattle. Durey and Nash were clambering up towards a massive slab of rock; its sides ridged and coloured, the rock jutted out from the wheatgrass.

'I followed Ike up here one day,' Nash said. 'There's a small cave under here,' he added, swinging the kerosene lantern as he went. He was panting heavily, the pain in his ankle making him break out in sweat.

'You could've just told me where the stash was, you know,' Durey suggested, gasping for breath as well. 'Save your ankle. I'd have brought it down for you.'

'I want to see it myself, Tom. Finders keepers.'

'Finders sharers,' Durey amended.

'Yeah, that's what I meant, Tom,' he said, slipping with his good foot down a small incline of scree and sending up small clusters of dust.

Durey followed cautiously and had to duck as the overhang approached.

Then they were in the shade and the

temperature dropped. Where the massive rock emerged from the earth there was the gaping black maw, the cavern entrance.

Nash put a match to the lantern and the cave walls turned dull yellow ochre. 'Come on, Tom. We've hit pay-dirt — the stash is still here!'

Scrambling after him, Durey entered the cavern and grunted. Two large ammunition chests were tucked under a stone ledge to the right. 'What's in them?'

'Have a look-see, Tom. Then you'll believe me!'

Grunting because the confined space meant he had to crouch double to move at all, Durey slithered over to the nearest of the two. The hasps didn't own any padlocks. Durey lifted the lid and whistled. 'Jeez, you're right, Ed. This will set us up for life, I reckon!' He ran his hand through the gold coins. 'Damn, my back's aching already. Let's get the stuff out to the wagon and divvy it up!'

'OK, Tom. Bring that one now, we'll

come back for the other.'

Between them, they hauled the chests out of the cavern, up the scree, scrabbling and slipping. It took them well over two hours to drag the containers to the wagon, by which time they were exhausted.

'I reckon we should get away from here before we divvy it up,' Ed suggested, drinking a ladle of water. 'Just in case Ike comes back.'

'Yeah, that may be for the best,' Durey agreed.

They heaved the chests into the back of the wagon.

'We'll find somewhere to camp for the night,' Durey said. 'And have a celebration drink or two.'

'Sounds good to me,' Nash said, grinning in anticipation of Durey's liquor.

★ ★ ★

'Sir, there's somebody outside to see you,' the nurse said, gently nudging Clyde awake.

He shook his head and groggily pushed himself out of the enveloping leather chair. 'What?' Then he remembered. 'Ellen — Miss Maxwell, is she going to be all right?'

'It's too early to say, sir. The young lady lost a lot of blood.'

'Yes,' he said impatiently, 'I remember the doc saying that. But will she be all right?'

'Doctor Wilson removed the bullet and she seems to be in a stable condition.' She forced a smile, as if that action was an unfamiliar effort. 'We're hopeful for a complete recovery.'

An enormous weight lifted from Clyde's shoulders. He gripped the nurse's upper arms and sighed. 'Thank God.' Then he recalled her earlier words. 'Did you say there was somebody outside for me?'

She nodded. 'Yes. He didn't want to come in.'

Was it Ike? Who else? He said, 'Thank you, nurse. I'll go see him now.'

Clyde hitched his gunbelt and stretched

his back and shoulder muscles which had not appreciated his sleep in that leather chair. As he approached the front door, he slipped off the leather restraint from the six-gun and pulled the weapon out. It was fully loaded. Now was as good a time as any to get rid of Ike, once and for all. If only I'd done it years ago, he thought.

He opened the door and stepped out but before his foot had landed on the boardwalk, he paused and gasped. It wasn't Ike at all. It was James Thorp, of all people.

Consciously closing his gaping mouth, he said, 'Hello, Thorp. I thought you were dead.'

'That won't be the first time you've thought that, will it, Clyde?'

Then Clyde noticed his sister standing just behind Thorp. Thank God she'd survived as well.

'Hey, sis! I'm glad you made it.'

She glared. 'You never even stopped to see if I was all right. Abe said you assumed I was dead!'

'Abe?' This was confusing now. 'What's Abe got to do with it?'

'He tried to rape me last night — *and* earlier today. Jim here prevented it both times.'

'Rape? Abe Dodds? You must be mistaken, Anna.'

'No, you're mistaken, Clyde,' Thorp said. 'Abe Dodds and Ed Nash did your bidding and tried to assault Anna!'

'*My* bidding? Come on, Thorp, I know you don't like me, but I would never want to hurt my sister!'

Tears glistened in Anna's eyes now. 'You murdered our parents, Clyde. You almost killed me — then pretended you'd saved me!'

Hazy grey memories surfaced but he pushed them away. They couldn't be his memories. He was going to marry Ellen and become a good and respected rancher. 'I think you're being a mite delusional, sis.'

'I tend to agree there, Clyde,' said Ike, stepping out of the shadows of the adjacent alley, his hands resting deceptively lightly on his belt-buckle. The handles of his two Dragoon Colt six-guns shone in the evening sun.

Clyde squinted. 'Ike, where the hell have you been?'

'I was true to my word, boss. I checked the road was OK. As it was, I came into town and had a bath and a shave.' He glared at Thorp. 'I needed to buy me a new gun too.' Turning back to Clyde, he said, 'I see you got Miss Maxwell into the doc. Were you in time?'

Clyde said, 'It's too early to say, but they think she might pull through.'

'I'm pleased to hear it,' Ike said, his lips twisting into the semblance of a grin, revealing his gold tooth. He turned to face Thorp. 'Now, isn't it about time you stopped bothering Clyde? Leave him be, maybe? Let bygones be bygones, why don't you?' His hands moved slowly to his side.

'Ike, I don't think this is a good idea,' Clyde said, glancing at Thorp's stony face. 'Thorp's already bested Jake and Will.'

Without taking his eyes off Thorp, Ike said, 'Jake and Will were never in my league, Clyde. You know that.'

'I know,' said Thorp. 'You shoot to kill. That is, when you're not riding down defenceless women and children.'

'That was an accident!' Clyde exclaimed.

'Shut it!' snapped Ike in warning.

Anna moved to one side, pleading to Clyde, 'You've got to stop Ike, for God's sake! Enough blood's been spilled, Clyde.'

Clyde ignored her and bent his knees in a ready stance.

'No, Clyde, not this way!' she said.

'Keep back, Anna!' Thorp ordered sternly.

Clyde reckoned that Thorp was always influencing Anna. Telling her what to think and do. Damn the man! He shouldn't have come back into her life! Everything was just fine until he showed up.

It happened so fast, those involved acted on an impulse that was very close to instinct.

Ike drew both guns and fired at Thorp but he was a fraction of a second too slow and Thorp's two Remington revolvers blazed three shells into Ike's chest and another into his mouth, sending the gold tooth into the dust. A single bullet from Ike's righthand Colt smacked into Thorp's left arm and spun him around. In that same instant, Clyde's detestation for Thorp surfaced into an all-consuming rage. He saw his old enemy wounded and drew his six-gun and fired. But Anna had perceived his intention and ran forward, crying for her brother to stop, but it was too late, his action irrevocable.

Clyde shot his sister instead of Thorp.

His gun smoking in his hand, Clyde wailed, 'Oh, God, what have I done?'

'The last thing you'll ever do!' Thorp replied in a deathly cold tone. Steadying himself, he shot Clyde in the forehead.

Clyde Comstock jackknifed backwards onto the boardwalk and jerked spasmodically for a second then lay still.

As the gunsmoke cleared, Thorp knelt beside Anna and his heart started beating again when he tore at her blood-covered bodice and realized that the wound was superficial, slicing into and rebounding off her ribcage. She was still bleeding, though. Ignoring the pain in his left arm, he lifted Anna and carried her up the steps, past her dead brother and barged into the doctor's hallway.

The face of the nurse was extremely pale, as if she'd never seen blood before. But in the last few seconds a great deal of blood had been spilled.

'She needs a doctor,' Thorp told the nurse.

Doctor Wilson stepped out of his operating room and took in the scene at once. 'Good Lord,' he said, 'is it open season on women all of a sudden?'

11

Too Many Obstacles

Thorp paced up and down the doctor's vestibule, his left arm bandaged, the sling discarded. He had no doubt that Anna would pull through. Of course there was always the risk of infection in the wound: he'd seen plenty of deaths caused by gangrene and diseased injuries during the war. But the doctor seemed competent and he was hopeful that she would make a complete recovery. What most occupied his mind as he trod backwards and forwards was the terrible fact that he had killed Anna's brother. No matter how the justification was presented, that stark reality was still staring him in the face. Had he done it purely out of self-preservation? Or was it anger at

Clyde for shooting Anna?

Possibly. But buried not so deep now was another reason for exacting what amounted to revenge. Could he even contemplate telling Anna what had happened all those years ago? If they were to have any future together, he might have to keep silent. And yet that raw pain had driven him on these past few years. That pain hadn't been assuaged by the deaths of Jake Long and Will Hanson. And now he could add the shooting of Ike Douglas and Clyde Comstock — more notches on his gun, if he'd cared to cut them. They said that revenge was a meal best taken cold. Instead of which, he had indulged himself in the white-hot heat of gunfighting. But not one of those deaths actually eased the ache.

He was sorely tired of fighting and killing.

'Mr Thorp?' said the nurse, breaking into his reverie.

He stopped pacing. 'Yes? How is she?'

'Both ladies are going to be fine,' she

said, and smiled tentatively. His presence sometimes did that — made people uncertain when expressing emotions in front of him. 'Miss Maxwell is still sleeping, however.'

He offered a smile but it was more like a grin, really. 'Thank you, nurse.'

'You can go in to see Miss Comstock,' she said, opening the door.

Now it was his turn to be uncertain. He didn't know how much Anna had taken in during the gunfight. Nagging at the back of his mind was the unmistakeable truth that he had done what he came to do. The town's sign would be reduced in its population count, he supposed, as he had predicted. Unless they didn't count those living in ranches. He shrugged off that pedantic thought as he walked through an unoccupied bedroom and out the double doors to the veranda where he found Anna sitting in a cane chair, enfolding herself inside a colourful Indian blanket. Not so long ago, she'd hugged his blanket. The sun was setting behind Grimm Mountain, streaks of grey cloud tinged with pink, while the mountain itself was red-rimmed.

'Hello, Anna,' he said. The ghosts of his moments of pacing still lingered. He felt they were hovering over his shoulder.

She looked up. Her face was wan, drained of the life he had seen in her before the shooting. Fleetingly, he despaired, recalling the men who had never recovered from either their wounds or the sights they'd seen during combat. God, don't let this happen to Anna, he prayed.

'How do you feel?' he asked.

She gave him a faint smile, more out of courtesy than from herself. 'I feel like I've been shot. It's a new experience for me,' she said, and a faint tinkle of light flickered briefly in her eyes. 'I hope I don't encounter it again.'

'Me too,' he said, feelingly. 'I don't think my heart could stand it.'

'Your heart?'

'I feared that you were fatally injured, Anna.'

She lowered her eyes. Her lashes were long, her cheekbones attractive. He felt a powerful urge to kiss her eyes, her cheeks. He took a pace closer and though he wanted to kneel beside her, touch her and comfort her, he refrained. He felt that there were too many obstacles — perhaps of his own making — in the way.

'I understand, Jim.' She lifted her eyes to his and the warmth that he had seen was no longer there. No anger. No hate. No warmth. 'I really do understand why you shot Clyde,' she said, and her voice cracked.

'Excuse me, Mr Thorp,' the nurse said, hovering at the door.

'Yes?'

'Miss Maxwell is asking about Clyde Comstock. She wants to see him, to thank him.'

Thorp's blood ran cold as he felt Anna's accusing eyes on him. 'I'd better see her,' he said. At the veranda door, he turned. 'I'll see you later, Anna,' he said, adding, 'if you want?'

'Yes, I want that, Jim.' Her smile was faint but he welcomed it. It was better than nothing. 'Now go to Ellen.'

The room's kerosene lamp was lit. Outside, it was already dark. Ellen Maxwell was propped up in bed and her face seemed to have even less blood in it than Anna's.

'Hello,' she said, her voice a little faint. 'Do I know you, sir?'

'No, ma'am. My name's James Thorp. I'm an old friend of Miss Comstock, Clyde's sister.'

'Oh, I see. Has Clyde sent you? Is he indisposed?'

'Well, Miss Maxwell, it's . . . '

'Come, sit beside me,' she interrupted and gestured at a chair by the bedside. 'You must be a friend of Clyde's, no? Strange, how he never mentioned you.'

'I'll stand, if you don't mind, ma'am.'

'Your face tells me something is wrong.' He nodded. Her lower lip trembled a little. 'What have you come to tell me?'

'I'm afraid I've got bad news. I can't dress it up in fine words, ma'am. Clyde's dead.'

She gasped and her hands screwed up the sheets and she stared at him through tear-filled eyes. 'No, I don't believe you!'

'Believe me, ma'am, it's true. I killed him because he shot Anna, his sister.'

'No — we were going to get wed!' She sobbed. 'You must be wrong!'

'I wish I was, ma'am.'

'You're lying, you're lying!' she wailed.

'He's telling the truth, Ellen,' Anna said at the doorway.

Thorp swung round but he couldn't move, his feet seemed stuck to the floor under the weight of guilt.

Anna glided over to the bedside and hugged Ellen.

'Clyde saved my life,' Ellen wailed, 'and now he's dead.'

An exchange of a brief telling look passed between Anna and Thorp. Clyde had also 'saved' Anna's life all those years ago, though he had been the cause of her near fatal malaise.

At that moment the doctor entered. 'Mr Thorp?' Thorp turned. 'I've checked the contents, as you asked.' Doc Wilson held up the laudanum bottle. He hesitated as he registered that all eyes were on the bottle, not him. Ellen's sobbing had grown muted, expectant.

'And?' Thorp prompted.

'There are strong traces of poison in the sediment,' the doctor said. 'I must admit that I don't understand how it could have gotten there.'

Ellen shuddered and broke into a fresh paroxysm of sobbing.

Anna glanced over her shoulder, said, 'Kindly leave us be, will you?'

Thorp and the doctor left the two women to grieve.

★ ★ ★

Their ride back on the next day was a sombre affair because both of them were immersed in their own troubled thoughts. The death of Clyde hung between them and neither knew how to handle it, let alone bury it.

Without comment, they passed the spot where Abe Dodds had met his death.

Anna wore Thorp's rain-slicker through the waterfall while he used the tarp sheet. As they wound their way down the mountain trail, it was as if they could hear echoes of their banter from yesterday, but now it seemed unreal, belonging to some other people.

Late in the afternoon, the town of Bethesda Falls was visible at last, the trail meandering amidst a series of shale outcrops and clusters of boulders.

'I'll go visit Ellen tomorrow,' Anna said, finally breaking the silence.

'That's neighbourly of you.'

'I have to attend the funeral anyway.' Clyde's funeral.

'Yes, of course. When do your classes start?'

'Not till next week.' Her smile was

thin and wan. 'I must admit, I've missed the children over the holidays.'

'They're a kind of extended family,' he suggested.

'Yes, they are. From the docile ones to the scallywags, I love all of them.'

He wanted to say that he felt sure her parents would be proud of her achievement in becoming a schoolteacher. But he knew that if he mentioned them then it would dredge up the memory of how they died and why.

'How many children do you teach?' he asked, feeling that he was on safe ground.

She glanced at him and her smile now had just a little pleasure in it. 'All told, sixteen. Different ages, of course. I start them as early as I can. I'm a great believer in that. Gives them an advantage, I reckon.'

Her voice held a hint of pride and he couldn't gainsay her for that. He was proud of her too. She'd handled the traumatic assaults from Ed and Abe with remarkable resilience.

'Education gives you freedom, I reckon,' he said.

'Yes, I hadn't thought along those lines before, but I guess it does. Freedom to make the right choices, perhaps.'

'I haven't always made the right choices, Anna.'

'In what way?'

'I chose to leave you and go to war. That was a big mistake. If I'd stayed, maybe things might have worked out differently.'

She leaned across the gap between their horses and touched his left hand that rested on his thigh. 'You can't go through life having regrets, Jim. You ride out the bad days and move on. Move on with your life.'

'That's what I'll do, I think. Move on. I've brought you enough grief for one lifetime, Anna.'

She pulled in her horse. Colour rose in her cheeks and the old fire was in her eyes again. 'Now hold on a minute, Jim Thorp!'

'What have I said now?' he asked, stopping alongside her.

'Clyde brought woe into my life. Not you, for heaven's sake! Even in death he's hitting at you, spoiling your life just like the spiteful brat always wanted to do.'

'Anna, I think you're overwrought. You don't know what you're saying. He was your brother, after all . . . '

'And didn't he play on that?' she interrupted. 'He lied through his teeth. He lied to poor Ellen too.'

Thorp's sorrel lurched drunkenly against Anna's horse and the loud crack of the rifle sounded a second later.

'Get down!' Thorp snarled, jumping out of his stirrups seconds before his horse hit the hard ground.

Anna dismounted and dropped to his side, behind the wounded sorrel. She'd had the presence of mind to hold onto the reins of her horse.

Hunched behind his wounded horse, Thorp pulled his rifle out of its scabbard and scanned the jumble of rocks and boulders between them and the town. 'Are you all right?' he asked.

'Yes.'

He suspected that she was lying. She appeared to be a little short of breath; he only hoped that the wound hadn't opened.

She caught his look of concern and rubbed her ribcage. 'It hurts bad, but don't fret. Your horse is bad, Jim. He's in pain.'

'I know.' He'd pinpointed the position of the sharp-shooter. Hiding in the cluster of boulders to the east, on the edge of that depression. Satisfied that they were not in immediate danger, he withdrew his revolver and placed it at the sorrel's head. 'Sorry, pardner,' he intoned, and put the poor critter out of its misery.

Scrabbling behind the body of the sorrel, Anna tugged on the reins of her horse as it started becoming fractious. 'Any idea who it could be?'

'Nope.'

'What are you going to do?'

'*You're* going to ride into town. I'll cover you. Get the deputy out here *pronto*.' She nodded.

He pulled out his fob watch and checked the time. 'Over an hour to dusk,' he observed.

She was trembling where she crouched, her eyes on him, listening attentively.

'Ride low in the saddle and kick for your life, Anna.'

'I don't like leaving you here,' she said, readying herself.

'Whoever it is, I'm sure they're after me, not you. I want you away from here and safe in town. Now go!'

Hastily, she kissed him and swung up into the saddle and winced at the effort. Then she whirled the horse away, towards town. In those same seconds, Thorp stood and poured a volley of shots from his rifle into the cluster of boulders, sending up clouds of rock chippings and dust.

His heart tumbled when he saw puffs of smoke coming from the ambusher's direction and Anna's horse stumbled and swayed. But it was a game critter and carried on, though it seemed to be running a mite slower.

He quickly sank back behind his sorrel just before two bullets impacted in the horse flesh.

12

That Tombstone's Getting Close . . .

'A horse for a horse, Thorp!' the shooter called.

Thorp recognized the voice at once. 'Durey, you bastard! Why kill an innocent animal?'

'Hey, I only winged the critter. You killed it! Now I've still gotta give you that whipping I owe you!'

Two more slugs sank into the sorrel and air hissed out of the punctured belly.

Thorp scanned the surrounding area. About five yards away to his right was a copse of pines. To his left, half-concealed in a swathe of wheatgrass, there was a skull and bones of a bison's skeleton. Directly in front of him was the trail they'd come down, totally exposed. Behind him, the cluster of boulders where Durey hid. Durey had chosen well, damn him.

The copse of spruce offered the best option. Sinking lower behind his saddle, Thorp cut loose a length of his lariat and looped it round the pommel and tied it to his rifle scabbard. Perching his hat on the scabbard, he elbowed his way towards his horse's head and threaded the rope through the bridle rings; just enough play, he reckoned. Now he crawled back to the tail end of his horse.

His greatest danger was when he stood up and started running. For that very brief moment he would be a sitting duck. He was hopeful that Durey wasn't so hot a shot with a moving target.

'You'd better get some more practice, Durey! You barely hit my poor dead horse. Tried shooting the side of a barn lately?'

Another fusillade of shots. The saddle jerked and he heard the stirrup and cinch being hit. Tugging at the rope, he managed to raise his hat above the level of the horse's neck.

Durey fired, ventilating the hat, and in that same instant Thorp hefted his rifle and unwound and sprang in the other direction, towards the trees. He didn't bother shooting back but kept zigzagging like a scared rabbit, all the while hoping Durey was lousy at hunting rabbits.

Thighs aching with the effort, Thorp was within a couple of feet of the first tree trunks when he decided he'd used up all his luck. So he dived headlong among the weeds and detritus of the forest floor. Not a moment too soon — chips flew off the bark of the nearest tree in front of him.

Thorp rolled, his weapons digging into his waist. The wound in his left arm opened and hurt like hell. He finally bumped into another trunk. Scrabbling round this, he stood up and darted further into the shadows of the copse. Bullets zipped by, slicing branches and leaves, but were no real threat.

At last he stopped and bent double, catching his breath. His left arm throbbed but he had to ignore it.

He withdrew his fob, pleased to see it was still working. God almighty, Anna had only left ten minutes ago! It seemed an age. It would take her at least fifteen minutes to get into town. Then she'd have to get the deputy and anyone else they could round up to get their horses. Say, another fifteen minutes. And fifteen to return. He squinted at the horizon glimpsed through the trees. Dusk was due in about thirty minutes. He had to stay on the defensive until then.

Thorp checked his ammunition. His Henry only had seven .44 rimfire cartridges left. The rest were in a box in his saddlebag. His belt and Navy six-guns had plenty but he needed to get much closer for them to be effective. It was tight spots like this when he thought of one day investing in a rifle and six-guns that used the same calibre cartridge; that would cut down on the hassle.

Leaning against a trunk, he aimed at the boulders and let loose two shots. The sharp recoil against his right shoulder felt good. Good to be alive. Good to be fighting back.

'You can't run forever, Thorp!' Durey barked. 'I'm coming to get you!'

Thorp moved from trunk to trunk, keeping the boulders in view. He could hear shouting and the cracking of a whip. Then the trundle of wagon wheels. Horses whinnied. A small covered wagon hurtled round the boulders, swerving and turning towards the trees. Durey was visible crouching on the seat, cracking his whip at the two horses that pulled the wagon.

Thorp aimed and fired twice but at that moment the wagon-wheels hit some rocks and lurched. Wood splintered off the seat beside Durey's thigh. The man yelped and tumbled back inside, out of sight.

Spooked by the rifle shots, the horses kept on coming, straight at the trees.

Firing twice more, Thorp shot the

left-hand critter. He hated doing it but at the speed they were approaching neither horse was going to come out unhurt. As the poor animal fell, the traces snapped loose and the wagon tumbled over, slamming sideways into two trees. Shrieking, the other horse broke free and dragged a splintered length of the shaft, clattering among the trees. Birds fled the trees in their hundreds, screeching.

Jogging to his left, Thorp circled through the trees, keeping his eyes on the area where the wagon had crashed.

He detected no movement but kept the rifle ready, even if it only had one shell left. Slowly, he approached.

Everywhere was a mess. Pots and pans were scattered everywhere, sections of wood jutted in all directions and torn canvas flapped. A pair of legs stuck out from bits of board, a pistol lying under one thigh, and next to them were what looked like two ammunition chests, one of which had burst open and spilled its contents. Jewellery, brass candlesticks, gold chains and coins spilled out of a split gunny-sack and littered the forest bed of pine needles and cones.

Lowering the rifle, Thorp withdrew his handgun and approached the body. He heaved the board off the man and knelt down amidst the discarded riches. He was surprised to see Ed Nash, still recognizable though his face had been seriously damaged since they'd last met.

* * *

Both Durey and Nash had drunk the liquor as if it was going out of fashion for most of the night, celebrating their good luck. They slept for the best part of the day and had splitting headaches when they finally arose.

The pair were rather delicate around each other, Nash complaining about the noise of sizzling bacon while Durey growled over the distribution of the contents of the chests.

'How come I only get one candlestick and you get two?'

'Because there's an odd number, Tom!'

'So? If I hadn't cut you loose, you'd be in the hoosegow by now!'

'Oh, here, have it!' Nash snapped and threw it at Durey.

'Don't shout, my head hurts!' Durey groaned.

Raising his hands in agreement, Nash said, 'Let's get back to town and clean up.' He grinned. 'Tom, I reckon we need some tender loving care from the hellcats at the Bella Union.'

'Now you're talking,' whispered Durey.

As the wagon trundled along the trail towards town, Ed cocked his pistol behind Durey's neck.

'What the hell is this?' Durey snarled, cracking his whip over the two horses.

'I've been thinking, Tom. I don't reckon you deserve all that stash just for cutting me loose.'

'This ain't a good idea, Ed,' Durey had growled.

'I reckon I could use this wagon, till my ankle mends. I'll pay you a little for it, eh? Drop you off on the trail. You can walk to town.'

'You couldn't have got to Ike's stash without my help, damn you!' Durey spotted a series of large stones on the edge of the track and gradually eased the horses to that side.

'Maybe, maybe not,' Ed mused when suddenly the wagon jerked to one side as the wheels mounted the stones.

Durey stood into a crouch and flung his big head back, full into Ed's face. He swung round as Ed squealed, concerned about his nose. In a flash, Durey's knife was out and sank into Ed's left eye. The six-gun clattered to the floor of the wagon.

Hurriedly grabbing the reins, Durey steered the wagon off the trail towards a collection of boulders in a small depression. This place had been used to fight off redskins when the town's first inhabitants had just arrived. He braked and cast about.

The ground was soft enough, he reckoned. He started digging a shallow grave beside some boulders. He'd cover it with a few large rocks to keep the coyotes away.

He was about to haul Ed's body out of the wagon when he heard horses approaching along the trail. He peered over the edge of the boulder and couldn't believe his luck. It was Thorp. 'This is my lucky day,' he murmured, and dropped Ed onto the floor of the wagon and grabbed his Hawken rifle.

★ ★ ★

Thorp knelt by the body of Ed Nash, his revolver cocked and ready. He had no idea why, but it looked as though Durey had killed him. But there was no sign of Durey, yet he'd been steering the wagon a few minutes ago. He must have jumped out, he reasoned, just about to stand.

Suddenly, a whip lashed out from the trees and expertly cut Thorp's right hand, disarming him. Before he could pull his other six-gun, Durey whipped his left hand, drawing blood.

'Not so clever with the words now, are you?' Durey wheedled, stepping into the open, his whip in one hand, a knife in the other. Resting against a treetrunk behind him was his Hawken rifle.

Crouched by the body of Ed Nash, Thorp reckoned he had little chance of drawing his gun or unfastening his whip; he massaged his hands and felt his fingers slipping in the warm blood.

'I could shoot you like the dog you are,' Durey said, 'but I fancy giving you a bit of your own medicine first. So unbuckle your gunbelt.'

Pulse racing, Thorp considered his position. He knew that Durey would use the whip regardless. But for now it might be prudent to go along with him. As soon as Thorp let his gunbelt drop at his feet Durey lashed out again, the whip cutting into Thorp's left shoulder, ripping away part of his sleeve and exposing the bandage.

'So you've been wounded, eh?' Durey laughed and lashed at the bandaged arm, drawing blood. 'That tombstone's getting real close, Thorp!'

'Maybe, but whose name is on it?' Thorp replied, his eyes narrowing. Ignoring the burning pain, he put up a forearm, as if to ward off the next blow. Out of the corner of his eye, he spotted a small pile of coins, near his right hand.

When the whip hit him again, he steeled himself and grabbed it and wrapped it around his left forearm while at the same time scooping up those coins with his right hand. He flung them hard at Durey's face and tugged the whip. The action unbalanced Durey, but he was big and heavy and wasn't going to fall over or drop the whip.

In a swift movement Thorp unwound and grabbed at his gunbelt but Durey yanked on the whip. Thorp wasn't able to get the revolver but he unsheathed his knife, instead.

'You did well to survive the wagon crash,' Thorp remarked. 'Shame about the horses.'

'They're only beasts of burden, Thorp.' He tugged on the whip but Thorp resisted.

They now circled each other, Durey gripping the whip's stock, the length of leather taut between them.

'You fancy your chances fighting Indian-fashion, eh?' Durey snarled, and wrapped the whip round his arm and tugged, shortening the length between them.

'You haven't got any Indian qualities, Durey. I wouldn't debase any Indian by comparing him with you.'

'Shut it, swine!' Durey pulled and feinted with his knife but Thorp was too quick and evaded the bigger man's bear hugs and swishing blade. As they circled, their feet scattered coins and precious items from Ike's hoard and kicked pine cones, needles and dust into Ed Nash's lifeless face. Neither talked now, they were too intent on finding an opening to kill the other.

Durey kept pulling on the whip, laughing, wanting Thorp within arm's reach. Thorp continued to elude him. But at each tug Thorp's left arm hurt worse than the last.

Circling, they sliced at each other and kicked at their legs, trying to gain any advantage, but neither drew blood or buckled to the forest floor.

It was starting to get dark now. Thorp reckoned the deputy would be out here in a few minutes. But that might be too late. Because Durey was stronger and wasn't losing blood.

The next time Durey pulled the leather taut between them, Thorp held his ground. Then he cut the whip with his knife. Durey stumbled backwards a pace or two, taken by surprise.

Thorp dived for Ed's corpse. Half under the dead cowpoke's arm was the man's revolver.

Growling, Durey flung his knife at Thorp and lunged at his Hawken, the whip still coiled round his forearm.

Thorp ducked the knife and grabbed Ed's gun. Turning on his knees, he cocked it and fired as Durey lifted his weapon.

Durey shuddered and dropped the rifle. He stared at Thorp, his half-closed eye sprouting tears. Then, his eyes blazing, he started walking towards Thorp, untangling the whip from his forearm.

Thorp fired again, the shot pounding into the big man's chest.

Durey staggered a backward step then stumbled forward, walking again towards Thorp, raising the whip, his eyes wild.

Down on one knee, Thorp steadied himself and fired at Durey's head.

The big man groaned and fell backwards and the ground shuddered where he landed.

Epilogue

'I haven't done so much doctoring in so short a time since we fought off the Indians,' Doc Strang said, washing his hands in a tin basin while his wife continued to apply bandages to Thorp's shoulder. The sheriff was still in a spare bedroom upstairs, recovering.

'I much appreciate it, Doc,' Thorp said.

'We both do,' added Anna, standing by the door to the surgery.

'I think you're needed in the parlour, dear,' Mrs Strang told her husband.

'Pardon?' She flashed a look to the door and the man and woman who seemed only to have eyes for each other. 'Oh, yes, of course. I'll make myself scarce for a while.'

When the doctor and his wife had left, Anna said, 'I'm sorry you lost your horse, Jim. Does that mean you'll have to stay?'

He stood up and started putting on the fresh shirt that Anna had brought from Widow McCall's.

'No,' he said. 'I actually bought a new horse a couple of days earlier. In a way, that's what that fight with Durey was about.'

'Oh.' She looked down, her cheeks flushing.

'Hey, I didn't say I wasn't going to stay here.'

She glanced up, puzzled. 'I thought . . . '

'It depends on you, Anna.'

'Why?'

'Well,' he said in a serious tone, 'you may look at me differently when I tell you.'

'Oh, Jim! What could you possibly tell me that would alter my feelings for you?'

'The woman and daughter Ike and Clyde rode down in Deadfall, they were my ma and sister.'

She put a warm consoling hand on his. 'Oh, how awful for you!'

'Yes.' He buttoned up the shirt,

tucked it into his waistband. 'That's what drove me on to find the culprits.'

'I can understand that, Jim.' She held his hands. 'I'm truly sorry Clyde was involved.'

He shook his head. 'In that showdown at Rapid Creek, maybe I could have winged Clyde, wounded him. I think I shot him because I reckoned he'd killed you. But what if I'd just wanted revenge for my ma and Beth?'

She let go of him and turned away, distraught at seeing the strain on his features. 'Lives can be full of 'what ifs', Jim. At this moment, I'm a little numb after everything that's happened. But I'm not a fool. I know you're good at what you do, but I also know that you're not a cold-blooded killer.'

'No, I'm not,' he said.

Standing behind Anna, he held her shoulders firmly. 'But I fear those doubts of mine will always drive a wedge between us.'

She twisted in his grip and looked up at him, her eyes glistening. 'Clyde mussed up enough of my life, Jim. I want you to stay. I want to hold on to you.'

He grinned and his features lightened. 'I'll need to go get my things. There's a wagon-load of stuff back home. I may be some time as I'll have to sell up the family home and land. Will you wait for me?'

Anna nodded. 'So long as it doesn't take another five years, James D. Thorp!'

She was crying as he kissed her.

* * *

As he rode the palomino out of town, Thorp recognized the livery man, Amos Jones, standing with a tin of black paint and a small brush. He was busy altering the number of the town's population on the welcome board. It was no longer 111; it had been amended to 107. Thorp reined-in.

'Morning, Mr Thorp.'

'Howdy, Amos. How many more jobs are you holding down?'

'Oh, this 'n' that. Keeps me out of mischief.'

Thorp studied the sign. 'That doesn't seem to add up to me,' he said.

Scratching his head, Amos shrugged. 'I don't do the sums, Mr Thorp. That's what the mayor told me.' He eyed Thorp's gunbelt. 'It would've been a mite lower,' he added meaningfully, 'savin' Mrs Dunbar had twins last night — girls.'

Thorp nodded. On the death tally were Mr Maxwell, Abe Dodds, Tom Durey, Ed Nash, Ike Dawson and Clyde Comstock. While the birth tally was much fewer, with Mrs Dunbar's two new daughters, maybe innocent souls weighed more. Some kind of balance, Thorp supposed.

'More children for the schoolteacher, in time, I reckon,' Thorp said, and turned his horse to ride on. Then a thought struck him and he halted and leaned down, saddle-leather creaking. 'Keep your paint wet, Amos, because I'll be back.'

'Yeah, but is that to lower or raise the total, Mr Thorp?'

Thorp grinned. 'I'm hanging my guns up, Amos. You can *add* me to the population, I reckon.'

THE END

We do hope that you have enjoyed reading this large print book.

Did you know that all of our titles are available for purchase?

We publish a wide range of high quality large print books including:
Romances, Mysteries, Classics
General Fiction
Non Fiction and Westerns

Special interest titles available in large print are:
The Little Oxford Dictionary
Music Book, Song Book
Hymn Book, Service Book

Also available from us courtesy of Oxford University Press:
Young Readers' Dictionary
(large print edition)
Young Readers' Thesaurus
(large print edition)

For further information or a free brochure, please contact us at:
Ulverscroft Large Print Books Ltd.,
The Green, Bradgate Road, Anstey,
Leicester, LE7 7FU, England.
Tel: (00 44) **0116 236 4325**
Fax: (00 44) **0116 234 0205**

BOTH SIDES OF THE LAW

Hank J. Kirby

A full hand in draw poker changed Hardin's life — and almost ended it. First there was the shoot-out with the house gambler. Then suspicion of bank robbery, enforced recruitment into a posse, gunfights in the hills and pursuit by both sides of the law in strange country. He'd never had so much trouble! What should he do? Drift on, away from this hellhole, or stay and fight? There was no real choice — it was fight or die . . .

LIZARD WELLS

Caleb Rand

After losing his whole family to a bloodthirsty army patrol, Ben Brooke takes to the desolate Ozark snowline. Years later, he returns to the town called Lizard Wells, where the guilty soldiers have degenerated into guerrillas, bringing brutal disorder to the town. Also living there is the tough Erma Flagg — and more importantly, Moses, a young Cheyenne half-breed . . . After a wild thunderstorm crushes the town, Ben, in desperate need of help, chooses to step single-handedly into a final reckoning.